The Commandments

of a

Female Hustler

2

by

Stacey Fenner

40,800 words

2016 Gray Publishing Paperback Edition

CONTENTS

Dedication 6

Acknowledgments 7

Chapter 1 9

Chapter 2 14

Chapter 3 19

Chapter 4 26

Chapter 5 32

Chapter 6 40

Chapter 7 47

Chapter 8 56

Chapter 9 63

Chapter 10 70

Chapter 11 77

Chapter 12 86

Chapter 13 95

Chapter 14 102

Chapter 15 109

Chapter 16 116

Chapter 17 122

Chapter 18 132

Chapter 19 141

Chapter 20 148

Chapter 21 155

Chapter 22 163

Other Books by Stacey Fenner 168

About Stacey Fenner 173

Visit Stacey Fenner's Facebook for the latest news and updates.

Instagram: authorstaceyfenner

Twitter: @sfenner1

Facebook: www.facebook.com/authorstaceyfenner

DEDICATION

This book is dedicated to my two daughters, Jasmine P. Elder & Janay L. Fenner.

My prayer is that neither one of you will ever find yourself in a position to become any one of these characters that I have written about in this book

Never sell yourself short of what God has designed for you both! Carry your morals with you, respect your character, and remember your life didn't come with a price tag on it!

ACKNOWLEDGMENTS

As always, first and foremost, I have to thank my Lord & Savior Jesus Christ for all the blessings and lessons that have come my way and continue to come my way. Thank you for your grace & mercy. This has been a trying year for my family and I!

Darin, I hope you're proud and I'm making you smile up there in Heaven! Love you bro, missing you every day.

I would like to thank every person that has ever read any one of my books. Thank you for your support, it means the world to me. Without you, I wouldn't be able to do what I love to, which is write.

Thank you to my husband, Mr. Keith Blackwell, for all that you do for me, and for keeping a smile on my face through some of my darkest moments.

Thank you to my wonderful parents, Lester & Paulette. Don't know what I would do without you! Mom, all I want is for you to be healed and living a healthy life.

Thank you to my two lifelines, Jasmine & Janay. Love you both to infinity. My lil Nook who brings me nothing but joy in my heart, G-Ma loves you!

Thank you to my wonderful family & friends that support me and continue to support me! I thank you a million times over!

A very special thank you goes out to George Sherman and the rest of the team at G-Street Chronicles, for believing in me, and the continued support! Teamwork makes the dream work!

CHAPTER 1

NINA

"Moose, who the hell shot Lala?" I needed answers as my panic mode set in.

"I don't know, but I'm going to get down to the bottom of this shit." Moose replied all nonchalant. *Doesn't he realize what just happened here or 'Oh, because it's not him, no big deal.'*

"Yeah, I know you are! We ain't having this! Somebody just lit a fire they can't put out! Matter of fact, Moose, let me handle this. I got this! What did the Doctors say?" *Moose was here before me so he should know something.*

"They said she's going to be okay. She got hit in the face at close range. They're working on her." Moose said shaking his head walking back and forth in the emergency room at University. Cops were swarming all over the place.

"Her fucking face? Oh my God, Moose!" My Lala! My Lala! I hope these doctors can work a miracle, but I'm going to love her regardless.

I told her that I wanted to move from Pennsylvania Ave., but she wanted me over there for business purposes. She got shot one block down from my apartment. I heard it, but it was nothing unusual. Happens all the time. It never dawned on me that it was her. She had just left my house. *I knew I should have gone with her! But no, she didn't want me to. I would have taken the bullet myself!* We don't even have any beef out here, it doesn't make sense. Everybody on the Ave. works for us. I have to get some more info but that will have to wait. My first priority is to be here for Lala. Everything else can wait. I sent out a text telling everyone cease all calls, I'm unavailable until I hit them back!

"Nina, I have some business to take care of. Hit me up when she gets out of surgery or whatever, and let me know what these scumbag cops are saying! Don't give them any information, play it cool, like we always do! I'm going to hit the streets to see what I can find out!" Moose said.

"Okay Moose, you do that! I'll hit you as soon as I hear something!" That's good. Let Moose find who did this and I will handle it when I can.

*****

I'm in love with Lala. There's nothing that I wouldn't do for her. She's my rock that's just misunderstood. Everyone thinks she's a straight up bitch, but I know her softer side. She does care; she has feelings, she just doesn't show them very often. We work well together on and off the streets; teamwork makes the dream work!

This takeover was one of the best things that could have ever happened to us. Beauty and brains…no dummies over here. The only issue we had at first was the male ego. Guys don't like taking orders from women, but Moose handled that. Now we get the utmost respect!

I've been ready to take my relationship with Lala to the next level. There's no reason why we should be living separately. We need a place of our own…out of the city. I don't want to work in the streets and live any place where we do business at. It's time for us to do this! Especially now; Lala is going to need me more than ever.

I've seen people that got shot in the face…it's not a good look. Even with this new technology there is no perfect fix. Lala lives off her beauty. I'm not sure how's she going to handle it or what her mental state will be like. Somehow we're going to make it through this. We have to.

*****

"I'm looking for the family of Lashay Valentino!" The doctor finally came out.

"I'm right here, Doctor." I walked over in a hurry to hear to some news.

"Hello, I'm Dr. Miller. I'm the plastic surgeon that got called in." He reached his hand out. "And you are?"

"Uh, I'm her sister, Nina! Nice to meet you, Dr. Miller. Is she going to be alright?" I asked looking for some good news.

"Well, she's going to live but her face is pretty much distorted. We did the best we could for now. She's going to need some more surgeries done. We have to let her face heal first then go back in. We were able to get the bullet out; the good thing is your sister is going to be just fine. She was shot at close range; that bullet could have easily gone straight to her head. I just want you and her to look at the brighter side of things. She will be in here for at least a couple of days. We will keep her under the 'Jane Doe' system. Anytime we have gunshot victims, it's hospital policy." Dr. Miller was explaining sounding very apologetic.

"Doctor, will her face ever be what it used to?" I need a little more understanding of exactly what Lala is facing.

"Well, I can't really tell you that right now, it's too early. I know that she's going to need some more reconstructive surgery. I will do the best that I can, but there are no guarantees and it's a lengthy process." Sounded like Doctor Miller was putting it mildly, kind of brushing me off and beating around the bush.

I hate when doctors don't give a straight up answer to the question, but I'll keep my cool. He seems to be a pretty okay doctor and he's sexy in his own right. A black, handsome doctor. I didn't see no rings. If it wasn't for me being in this relationship with Lala, I would fuck him! Never been with anybody with a PhD before. Might be kind of interesting to know what he can do in the bedroom.

"Thank you, Doctor. Can I see her?" I hope I'm ready and don't go in this room and spazz the fuck out!

"Yes, she will be upstairs in a room soon. The anesthesia hasn't worn off yet; she's going to be pretty much out of it for today. Let me take you back there. I have her face bandaged up, so you won't see any of her scarring. It's the right side; the left side of her face seems to be okay." Dr. Miller said as he was walking me back to see Lala. "Oh, we have restraints on her. We don't want her trying to mess with her face." Dr. Miller walked me back to the recovery room. "Here you go; she's in recovery room number two."

"Thank you again, Doctor!" I walked in the room figuring I could hold Lala's hand and talk to her for a while. I needed to let her know that I was here for her, but I guess these damn detectives had other plans for me. They were all over me asking questions like I was the one that shot her.

CHAPTER 2

JAY

I really wish my life wasn't so complicated all the damn time. Why do bad things keep happening to me? I can't win; I'm sick and tired of being sick and tired. Every time I turn around it's something.

Boss and his crazy, sick ass is addicted to every drug out there on the streets. One day he's flying around with his eyes popping out his head, the next day he's nodding, and then I catch him swallowing pills! Enough!

This nigga went from having it all, to rock bottom in a split second, and he was taking me right with him. Not that I get high, but he was stealing everything in sight, even down to every piece of jewelry that he ever bought for me or himself. I come home and T.V.'s are missing from out of every room. Then my dumb ass goes and replaces them, only for him to steal them again. He was stealing my money, maxed out my credit cards, sold my car up from underneath me, knowing that I'm taking care of his kids. I tried my hardest to hang in there. Because I'm from the streets of Baltimore, I can just about handle anything. I understand he's addicted, but get some help. I paid twice for him to go to rehab. Fool didn't last a week after he begged me to pay for it. I should have gone with my instincts. You can tell when a person is ready or not.

He wasn't paying any bills at all. We got evicted from our mini mansion; it was too much for me to handle all by myself. I sold what little furniture we had left from Boss's thieving ass. When I came home to an empty living room and kitchen I couldn't believe my eyes. I thought we got robbed. Called the cops and everything, but there were no signs of any robbery. The police and I were looking back on the camera and it was Boss, plain as day, coming in the house with some middle-aged couple showing them the furniture, and the couple was smiling from ear to ear. He probably sold it for pennies compared to what it was worth. About an hour later the truck pulled up and they hauled out the furniture, handing him an amount of money that only his eyes could see.

He set me up good that day because he knew I would be gone all day. I had to take Grams to the doctors, plus beat two faces. The police said there was nothing that I could do about it. I already knew that, but I was so mad I wanted his ass to get arrested anyway.

Since I couldn't do things the legal way, I figured I'd do things my way! I drove around and finally found him walking down

Wilshire Boulevard with some cracked up bitch, looking like a used up piece of shit. I approached him on some angry woman shit, calling him and her every word but the child of God!

One, I'm mad at myself for giving him the benefit of the doubt. He called himself trying to play me like a fiddle. My intentions were not to go there, but disrespect I will not tolerate. He told me that my job was done and to go back where I came from, that the furniture was his so he could do what he wanted to do with it.

I started swinging on him, tearing his high ass up giving him blow for blow, and old cracked out bitch started running off at the mouth like she was about that life. *Hmmm, I fooled her!*

I politely strutted back to the car and grabbed my ponytail holder, put my hair in a ponytail and went to work on that ass. All my frustration got taken out on her, anger boiled in my soul! All she had to do was keep her rotten ass mouth shut! Here I am, taking care of kids that I never pushed out my pussy, that belong to him and Tasha and he thinks he can treat me any kind of way! All I heard was, 'Stop it, Jay. Stop it, Jay!' *Yeah nigga, no more bodyguards for him. He's lucky if he weighed a buck fifty.* Food wasn't his friend these days.

*****

I had to uproot the kids and move across town where it was much cheaper. It was still a nice neighborhood. Now we're in Lakeland; I refuse to live in anybody's hood. If I can save these kids from experiencing half of what I been through then that's what I plan to do. Now I'm paying three g's a month versus ten g's a month for rent. It's only a three bedroom, but we're adjusting to living in smaller quarters. It's just taking some time to get used to.

At first I let Boss come with us. Bad mistake. He started stealing the meat from out the freezer and that was it! Grams called me up when she went to take something out to eat and the freezer was empty. The kids had been in school, Grams was in her room and I had to beat faces for a video shoot that day, so somewhere between A and B, he robbed us of the food. Now he's resorted to taking the food that I use to feed his kids with. That's because I had everything else on lock-down.

My apartment looked like Fort Knox…locks on everything! I had to; Boss had become your twenty-four hour thief. Whatever he could get his hands on he was stealing it! He even stole the kids PlayStation, Wii, and Xbox…plus the games. It got to the point where I was losing sleep, up trying to watch him and happy when he wasn't home. The problem was, we never knew when he would pop up to get some sleep.

I got my key back to the apartment one night when he was sleeping. As much as I asked for it, he wouldn't do me the honors. I had my locks changed too, you can never be too careful when it comes down to him. He had leverage over the kids; regardless he was still their father so they didn't even have keys. I already knew that his manipulating self would try one of them. I sat the kids down, explained to them in a very kid friendly way that their father is sick and wouldn't be able to be an active parent in their lives, not that he ever was. I called Tasha, explained the whole scenario to her, figuring that she would come get her kids. Wrong thought. She said she was coming, three months later, still haven't seen or heard from her! She even changed her number. Neither the kids nor me have any way of contacting her! *She's so trifling; I swear some people don't deserve to give birth.*

*****

Boss beat everyone in the industry, never made good on money that was due to them. All of his artists were on the hunt for him. Now I'm stuck in the middle of his bullshit and my clientele has damn near come to a halt. Being with him had messed up my credibility.

Work is slow. I'm barely making ends meet. *Back to robbing Peter to meet Paul!* I've resorted to going back to my old ways. It's not something that I'm proud of, but yes, I'm fucking for money! It's the only way I know, and these men in L.A. have no problem paying my type of price!

CHAPTER 3

CHESAPEAKE DETENTION CENTER

"Inmate number 919737, let's go! You have a visitor!" Mean ass correctional officer Jackson said. I can't stand her she always has an attitude. I think she needs some dick or something. She's been mad every day since I've been in here.

*****

It's about time that somebody came to see me. Moose probably sent someone for me, my man! Moose owes me an explanation! I knew he would come through! I want to know how we all end up in here, and he manages to duck out the whole situation. He could have at least warned me. Time must not have allowed him. *It's a good thing; both of us didn't need to be in here.* One of us needed to be out there making sure shit was right in them streets. Being behind these bars was brutal. I handle myself well in here though. I knew a lot of these cats in here anyway. There wasn't too many willing to try me, only that damn Sweets and Rock.

We couldn't even pass by each other without throwing some blows. We spent more time in the hole than out here with the population. The Warden finally figured out that it was best to separate us. Sweets was on one side, Rock was on his side, and me on my side. It cut down on the confusion between us three.

Rock still had it in for me for murdering his cousin Tiz, but I told that nigga it's a bunch of hearsay. Come to me with some proof! Every time I saw Sweets he blamed me for what happened and I blamed him. He thought it was somebody from my camp, but I think it was somebody from his camp. The way we run things, wasn't nobody willing to turn on us.

*****

I can't wait to see who my visitor is. I'm out of touch with the outside and it don't feel too good. The only phone number I remembered by heart was Diamond's and she hung up on me three times; screaming, hooping and hollering about how I should have listened to her. Don't nobody want to hear that when they locked the fuck up! It states the obvious, so I just stopped even trying to call! I knew it would only be a matter of time before somebody showed up.

*****

When I reached the visitor's area I see Diamond sitting and waiting on me, looking pretty as fuck! *Aww shit! My dick is getting hard and I'm smiling from ear to ear.* I wanted to haul ass over there, but had to keep up with my rep. *My baby came to see me!* I sat down across from Diamond grabbing both her hands.

*****

"You finally decided to come see a nigga?" The smile on my face was so warm that butter would melt. I'm so happy to see her. Had I'd known this I would have had my boy Koosh give me a haircut and shape me up. I'm looking rough.

"Yeah well, you lucky I'm here at all. After I calmed myself down from being mad at you I decided to take a drive." Diamond said smiling. *She never could stay mad at me for long.* "How are you doing in here?"

"I'm hanging, trying to maintain. I'm missing and thinking about you every day of course!" I shrugged my shoulders. "The Feds are fucking me over. Still no court date; dragging this thing out! I still have no bail hearing when I'm not a flight risk! They know what they're doing. Trying to keep me in here while they're building a tight case."

"Swift, I miss you. I just wish you were in North Carolina with me! I wanted to show you something different!" Diamond said with tears in her eyes. "This is what I was afraid of. I never wanted to come here and see you locked up like some animal."

"I know, baby, but what's my name? I got this name because of how I move! You don't think I've been in here without thinking of a master plan to get the fuck out of here! Save those tears for the happy ones when I get out!" *I'm even more confident now about getting out of here, now that I can have Diamond doing the work I need done on the outside. I should have known she was coming, but a part of me was thinking she said, 'Fuck him!'*

"How? They have so much evidence against you, it almost like you're never getting out!" Diamond said wiping her tears away. "What do you need me to do?"

"I need for you to get me a lawyer. Call Attorney Philstein, he's crooked as hell. That's the same one that handled all the paperwork for me on the condo and car that was in that bitch's name. If he can't represent me then he knows somebody that will. They had this Public Defender trying to take over my case. I refused and told her she better get the fuck out my face! I wasn't putting my life in her hands. Let him know that I need another bail hearing as soon as possible. When I get out on bail, between the lawyers and the feds, this will be held up for at least a couple of years. Then I'll go from there, straight like that!" I had to calm Diamond's nerves down a bit. Letting her know, I'm getting out of here!

"Okay, I will take care of that as soon as I leave here. Make sure you call me tonight. I will have some information for you!" I could tell that Diamond was getting anxious to get out of here, but hell no! I want every second of my visit.

"How's your pockets, doing? I got plenty of money stashed. The Feds didn't seize it all!" *Yep, I have a few hiding spots that don't anybody know about.* If Diamond's money gets low, she's straight. I just don't want to tell her where they are, just yet. Some secrets I need to keep.

"I'm good for now. You know I'm not a big spender. The Feds were questioning me all the way down there in Carolina. They seized my bank accounts and took the cars, but my accounts finally got released. You know me, wasn't much in there anyway! I always just stacked the cash that you gave me! I don't know when or if they will give back the cars, but it's okay. I went and got me a little, black Honda Accord. It rides pretty nice too." *Diamond is so humble. It never did take much to please her.*

Diamond was smarter than I thought. When I was giving her money I thought she was spending it all up. She must have a nice, little, pretty bit stacked up. Good for her, smart move! I shouldn't be surprised. I've never fucked with a dummy! Even that bitch, LaLa was smart in her own way, as much as I hate to admit it.

"Yeah well, you're getting your car back and mine too, once you get in touch with the lawyer. They were in your name. All I did was drive them every now and then. Trust me, this attorney will come up with a good ass story. Dude is amazing! That's why he stays on my payroll." *I hate how the system works. They can just go take people's shit! What I have shouldn't even matter in a court of law. This is not Divorce Court.*

"Swift, I don't want it. You gave that car to that bitch then gave it to me!" Diamond does have a point. I'll just get her an Infinity or something. Either way, she ain't riding around in no Honda. She's a Diamond and will get treated like one.

"Has anyone been putting money on the books for you?" Diamond asked.

"Nah, but I'm good! I get just about everything I need and want in here. My name speaks for itself. Somebody is always looking out for me. I'm surprised that Moose ain't holding me down right now! Can you find out what's up with that?" Moose was breaking the code. I even had a few of these cats come up to me and ask why they haven't received anything on their books. He knows that we take care of all of ours…unless money is low. *Or he might be locked up somewhere else.* Diamond will find out for me.

"First of all, Moose should have been in that warehouse with y'all. You put too much trust into your boys! Now his ass ain't even trying to take care of you while you in here! Wait until I see him. I'm gonna ask him like, 'Nigga what's really good?' He didn't even hit me up to see if you were alright…if you needed anything. Then when I tried to call him to see if he had any more information than the news, his phone was off or the number is changed." *Diamond is feeling some kind of way, that's my baby. I feel exactly where she's coming from, but I'm giving Moose the benefit of the doubt.*

"Maybe he is locked up. His phone wouldn't be off! I need you to find out what's going on!" *If Moose ain't out there, then who the hell is?*

"Okay. I'll see what I can dig up out here!" Diamond smiled.

"Two minutes left and your visit is over! Let's rap this up folks!" the CO yelled.

Damn, already? When you're behind bars you never want a visit to end. "Alright baby, I'll call you tonight!" I gave Diamond a kiss that could last a lifetime. "Do me another favor please?"

"What's that?" Diamond asked.

"Keep that thang of mine tight!" I laughed as I watched that ass just a jiggling as she was walking away. A nigga can't wait to get out of here! It's a catch twenty-two. You want your girl to visit, but don't want to see her leave. The life behind bars, waiting on an out!

CHAPTER 4

LALA

I've been home a whole week and Nina wouldn't leave my side. *Like I'm some weak bitch that would do something to myself.* I'm going to be stuck here on the inside of this apartment until my face gets fixed.

Dr. Miller was cool, but he has to do better than this. When he took the bandage off I passed out three times just from looking at it. My face looks so damn distorted that you can't even recognize me. I keep the bandage on to keep from having to look at myself. Nina tried putting some makeup on me but it didn't work. *I need a miracle right now. I can't walk around as an ugly bitch!*

Dr. Miller said I have to have a couple more surgeries within the next six months. I wish he could do it now! I want my face fixed and he talking about, 'ain't no guarantee he can get it to look a little better!' *That's not gonna cut it!*

I have Nina calling around to the best of the best, even they're saying that it could take years, but they can't guarantee anything either. All I keep doing is crying. It's hard for me to shed real tears, and no matter how many times Nina keeps telling me I'm beautiful to her, it don't mean shit to me! All I see is ugly, ugly, ugly!

*****

I made Nina take down every mirror in here except for the one in the bathroom. I can just avoid that one. I can't even look at myself! These bitches have one up on me now, but believe me, I'm determined to be beautiful again. My looks got me to where I am today! I feel like an injured athlete that can't play anymore. I worked so hard to keep my face and body intact, for what? To look like this?

*****

Leroy has been ringing my phone off the hook. *I can't deal with him right now!* For one, I can't get rid of Nina, and for two, I have no intentions on letting him see me like this! Nina still thinks he's just my trainer. She has no idea that I'm fucking the old man! *She will have a fit and probably shoot him dead!* She has a love for me that's beyond obsession. I can do no wrong in her eyes, even when I hurt her feelings. She's like a hardheaded kid that never gets enough!

Leroy has a bad habit of thinking he can just pop up. The last time he did it I popped up at his house to teach him a lesson. I even sat down and had a nice conversation with his lovely wife. She's a mentor for young women on the move, so I finagled my way right in the door. She actually liked me, which was a first. Said she saw a lot of herself in me. She's such a nice woman and wasn't even intimidated by my looks. She's a very confident woman.

I enjoyed startling him and making him sweat. He wasn't sure what was going to come out my mouth. I even stayed for dinner; the woman can cook too. Leroy was happy to see me leave. His face was so relieved. Lucky for him, I like his wife, and planned on using her mentorship to my advantage. That was before I got shot in the face!

I got to meet Diamond's so-called siblings. They seem like a close-knit family that has it together. I could tell that Diamond was cut from a different cloth. She didn't fit in with this family! I felt like I was watching the *Cosby Show*, that's just how they carried things. It was hard to tell if Leroy and his wife were fronting for the kids or if the shit is real. However, they make family life look damn good.

*****

"La, what are you thinking about?" Nina asked.

"Life, that's all!" It's two in the afternoon and I have yet to get up. By now I would have gotten up, ate, worked out, been dressed for the day and handled most of my business. I'm always on the go.

I guess depression does exist. I always thought people be lying and attention seeking, like what could be so bad about life? Now I see they really don't be exaggerating. I keep telling myself that I'm locked up with a release date somewhere in the future.

"It's going to get better, babe. I have to take you to see Dr. Miller tomorrow, and hopefully he will give you some good news." Nina slid in the bed next to me rubbing my leg.

"Stop touching me!" I yelled. "You always so horny. If you need some that bad then go out there and get you some!" Bitch gets on my nerves. Most days I just want her to go home, unfortunately I need her right now.

"You need to stop pushing me away! I'm trying to help you by relieving some of that stress! You need your clit licked!" Nina rolled back on the other side of the bed.

"I don't want to be touched right now; when and if I do, I'll let you know!" Nina tried this shit when I was in the hospital. Who does that? Always thinking that sex is a cure for everything! Find a cure for my fucking face that's all I want her to do!

"How long do you think that you can stay curled up in a fetal position? You do know that this process could take years right? What's the plan, Lala?" Nina was sounding a bit irritated. "Staying away from the streets too long is only going to damage business! I didn't help you build this empire to watch it burn down in hell!" *Help me, is she for real right now? All she did was make sure Sweets went to that warehouse and hit my phone when he left. All credit belongs to the one and only, me.*

"What the fuck do you want me to do? You expect me to go out here looking like this!" I pointed to my face. "Nobody will even recognize who the hell I am! I have to do things from the inside. Everything else you will have to do! I'll just set everything up for you!" Business was the last thing on my mind.

"Okay, consider that handled. Now let's talk about my real question, the one you've been avoiding giving me the answer to! Who did this to you and why? That detective called for you again today!" *I knew Nina wouldn't leave this alone for long. I may be able to toss her away sexually, but she won't sleep until she knows the truth!*

"You just stick to the script and tell the truth, just like you did when they came at you! Leave all of your unanswered questions to the detectives to figure out." *Leave it alone Nina, I got this all covered in due time.*

"Why the fuck should I wait on the detectives like I'm some outsider? Just like the police, I don't believe that you don't know who shot you! Whoever did it was standing in your face! Spill it Lala! Why would you protect someone that has you not wanting to look at yourself?" *Nina's right. Even if I don't tell the police, she deserves to know the truth.*

"Remember that side deal I made with Wex?" Wex was pushing pills and I agreed to let him sell on our territory for a small profit.

"Yes, I remember!" Nina was with me when I made the deal.

"Well, Moose found out about it and felt like I crossed him. When I left your apartment he was on the corner waiting for me. He flagged me down and I thought it was strange because nigga don't fuck with the West. He usually lets me do all the dealings. I'm thinking that something must have gone wrong. I pull over and he snatches me up, and brings me in that alley where all the abandoned houses are at. He was talking real grimy towards me. Talking about 'Bitch you gonna learn today! I'm not Sweets, Rock, or Swift! You can't knock me out the game. Since you think you slick, I got something for you!' He pulled out his gun and shot me! He thinks I'm scared of him and that's what I want him to think! I got something so sweet coming his way; he thinks he fucked up my face, he hasn't seen nothing yet! TORTURE IS COMING FOR MOOSE!"

Chapter 5

Jay

I dropped the kids off at school and headed happily to the airport to pick up Binky. She was free and clear, so now she was able to move around. I'm definitely looking forward to hanging with my girl and being able just to see a familiar face. We talk all the time, but it's nothing like her being here in the flesh! Binks has been the one listening to me. I call her with all my problems, but she be ready to take it the streets all the damn time! She wants to kill Boss, strangle Tasha, and shoot everybody in the industry for not messing with me! Off the hook she is, but that's my bestie, and we don't play about one another! Thank God this will be a permanent move. She can sleep right in the bed with me until we can do better. *I could use her help down here.*

I'm working on getting back on, and since she can do hair, that's just another asset that we have to offer. I'm going to hit up the gram, twitter, and book to start running some specials, see how it turns out. My name is already known and I don't have any bad reviews. I have a good feeling about this, especially since Bink is coming with something different. You haven't had a hairstyle unless you've had one from B-more!

I told Bink she needed to take pictures of all the heads she was doing to help build up her portfolio. This weekend we'll be hanging out networking, trying to gather up some business. I still have a few connections from Boss, so I know what's happening and where we need to be.

Grams is on point to keep an eye on the kids for me, which makes me free to do whatever. I'm ready; I haven't done anything in months without the kids anyway. I plan outings with them once a week. Sometimes I might miss a week, but I make up for it. That's the one thing that they have to look forward to. If they're doing what needs to be done in school then they deserve to be rewarded. It makes them think twice before they get it twisted. My program is working; the teachers have nothing but good things to say about them.

*****

I pulled up to the airport and I spotted Binky right away. My goal was to beat her here, but the plane must have landed a little bit early. I jumped out and ran over to my sister gal hugging and kissing her like we were a couple. *So excited and happy to see her.* On a positive note, now I have something to look forward to…our own salon. J&B's, offering a full spa day along with daycare services. There are a lot of single mothers that are unable to find babysitters while they are getting pampered. We're going to give L.A. a run for their money while we make them dollars! A real and legitimate female hustle.

*****

"Damn! Yeah, you missed me!" Binky laughed while helping me put her luggage in the trunk. *I hope she shook this stuff out, the last thing I want to see is a roach!*

"I sure did, lost without you! You know I don't rock with these hoes here! If it ain't business, then we ain't rollin!" I can't afford to get caught up in some bitch shit. Less is more; I can't take a chance on getting close to someone that has bad intentions. My tolerance level won't allow it, so it's best for me to stick with what I know.

"Well I'm here now and hopefully for good! From the moment I stepped on the plane it was a feeling of something so right! Like I'm ready to do this, get our own money! I have my portfolio, ended up running a half price right before I left to get them pictures, girl! Girl, that apartment was packed. Unc was in his glory watching all them females. Jay, stuff in B-more is real crazy right now that I'm so focused on doing better!" Binky started rolling a blunt. *Now I know this chick didn't get on a plane with some weed. That could have been another charge.*

"Binky, why in the hell would you take a chance like that? You could have been detained with another charge!" She's over here talking all good about getting this business up and running, but coming off the plane with a blunt on deck. I'm going to have a nice little conversation with her, she can't just talk about doing better, she has to show it.

"Jay please, I got this from some dude that was in the airport trying to holla at me! I wouldn't risk going back in the system for some weed. We got plans and goals to accomplish. Trust, I'm on point! I know that look that you're giving me!" *Whew, that was a sigh of relief. Binky is talking my language.*

"How's my favorite Uncle taking you leaving him?" I swear her Uncle is the strangest man, but the realest. *He has to be feeling some kind of way. I hope he's not mad at me for taking Bink away.*

"He wasn't okay at first, but once I told him to let me get on and I'm sending for him, getting him right out them projects, just like you did for Grams! After I said that, he was asking me, 'When you leaving?'" *I needed that laugh; I can see his half of a smile and hear him asking her that too.*

"So, what's going on at home? I know we've been mostly focused on my hell, but I could use some gossip right now!" B-more, for me, is a place that I rarely think about. After Jock's funeral did me in, I try my best to erase that place from my mind. It holds too much pain for me. Now that I have Bink here with Unc on his way soon, there's no need for me to even visit anytime in the near future. L.A. is my home for now, and where I plan on building.

"Well for starters Lala got shot in her face; I heard it can't be fixed either! I almost ran up to the hospital to check on old girl, then I thought about me putting my foot up her ass and decided against it. I have no love for the girl! She should have never carried us the way she did!" Binky has a bad habit of rehashing the past. I haven't forgotten what Lala did, but all is forgiven on my part. I don't hold grudges, it only stops my growth. I'm in a different state of mind when it comes down to stuff like that.

"Wow, I know she's losing it!" Lala only had beauty to stand on, now what? *Now she will find out that looks ain't everything.* I'm at a loss for words. "Who did it?"

"I don't know, but I told you that Moose was the one that set up Swift, and from what I heard, Lala was about that plot too. If that's true, it could have been anybody."

"I still can't believe that Moose would do something like that! I would have never thought that of him! Now La, on the other hand, I can picture it!" *You can't trust nobody these days. People will turn on you in a sec just for some power.*

"Yeah well, we didn't think Lala was capable of doing us wrong but she did! We have to make a pact that no matter what, to never go there with one another. Your loyalty to me, means the world. Can we add another commandment?" Binky laughed, but she was dead ass serious. *Here we go with this commandment stuff. I thought we got rid of that brainwash right along with Lala.*

"Huh, yeah, the one that Lala forgot to add in there when she was making up her do's and don'ts! She's a straight up idiot! I will never turn on you, I'm riding with the Bink! You have my word on that!" I said while looking at all the rush hour traffic up ahead that we were going to be stuck in.

"Well good, now I have something else to tell you. I've been thinking about this business venture…how about we just open up a shop?" Binky asked.

"Yeah, that's the ultimate plan. First we have to get the money up! Start off small and then we can open up a shop. You need to get your license." Bink doesn't realize that it takes a lot to open up a business. It's not something that happens overnight. You can't just pick a spot and say, 'I want to do business there.'

"We have the money and then some. Whatever we want to do, we can." What the hell? Where did Binky get money from? I've been helping her and she's been stashing. I've been giving her my last. Spreading my legs, on my knees for some dollars to just to make ends meet and to be able to send her some of my hard earned money. Oh hell naw, I'm not feeling this!

"Wait a minute!" I pulled over so that I can make sure I'm hearing right. "Let me get this straight, you had money all this time?" *Bink has some explaining to do before I go any further.*

"Nope, I wouldn't do that to you. A couple days ago I was chilling with Moose. I found out where he stashes his money. He started bringing me to his house, finally. Like I didn't know he had a few. I don't know why he plays me, of all people, for a fool. I noticed that every time we go to his house he runs down into the basement and then comes back upstairs. We got drunk, well he got drunk; I already knew what I was up to. He goes to sleep after I rode him to bed, and I dipped into his stash. This nigga got hundreds of thousands dollars that he's sitting on. Peep this, two days before I asked him for five hundred, just to see what he was going to say. He tells me wait until Friday and he will see what he can do! At this point I'm tired of always waiting to see what he can do, so I'm going to take mine. That's when I made my escape plan and just took what I thought was feasible enough for all my services that I provided for him! I played it off though. Made sure he woke up from his drunk sleep with me laying there, butt ass naked, fake snoring and all. He woke me up and said it was time to go. Now I always bring my duffle bag with overnight clothes, just in case. I filled that bitch up like my life depended on it! When I tell you it was an easy transaction, it went so smooth! He dropped me back off home a rich bitch!" *Am I hearing correctly? Binky has truly lost it. Everybody knows you don't fuck with Moose and his money.*

Binky was still rambling on about how she deserved this money and the whole time I'm thinking, OH SHIT! She needs to give him back every dime before Moose is standing in both our faces! What does she have me involved in now? I don't want any fucking drama around me, the kids, or Grams! Then she fly's down here like he can't find her ass! Oh hell to the no! "Binky, what in the hell were you thinking? Give Moose back that money before he comes looking for me and you! Out of all the stupid things you have done in your life, this one right here, tops all of them!"

"I'm not giving him back shit! The way I see it, we even. That nigga ain't coming nowhere. He's going to stay his ass right there in B-more! You think he's going to come all the way to California on a goose hunt, for some money he can get back in a day? I highly doubt it. Come on now, we're talking about Moose. He ain't never been out of the state of Maryland!" *Binky was underestimating a man that loves money more than he loved himself.*

"You emptied out your bag of overnight clothes in his basement and filled it up with money, letting Moose know that it was you that took his fucking money! A drunk man can miss a dollar or two from his wallet, it's an easy getaway! I do it all the time. You might have even been able to throw him off track if you didn't leave your name all over it." *This is some crazy shit right here, Binky can get her ass killed. Stealing from a drug dealer is never a good outcome. Not only does this involve me, but Grams and the kids too! I can't take no chance, especially when lives are at stake. Of course, if it was just me, then me and Bink could stay on the run, but that isn't my life!*

"Well I got us a little over a hundred and I hid my clothes. He won't find them!" Binky said all excited. Binky has to get her ass back on a plane to B-more and sneak that money back to Moose somehow, then come back. We will make it on our own, not on some stolen money that don't mean us no good! Moose is not letting that slide. For that kind of money, he will be on plane. Just like a track player running in the Olympics.

CHAPTER 6

CHESAPEAKE DETENTION CENTER

"I'm sorry Ole G, I fucked up and got involved with the wrong muthafuckers!" Sweets was having a visit that he wasn't looking forward to. "I'm working on an inside plan to have Swift's ass deleted altogether."

"So Swift is the one that set all this up, but his ass in here too? That's bullshit! He didn't do this! He's much smarter than that. Come again with something better than that stupid shit that's coming out your mouth! There's no way he would stop his money flow!" Ole G was coming at me hard.

"Look, Swift was trying to set us up and he got set up in the end. His plan backfired on him! I talked to Rock and he thinks the same thing! He had to be planning a takeover. I'm just waiting on you to give me the word and he can be handled today, if that's what you want!" Sweets put on an evil grin looking up in the air then bowing his head.

"Did you hear what I said fool? That doesn't add the fuck up! Don't be trying to feed me on what you think! Moose is the leak, dumbass! Who do you think took over? He's the one that set all y'all dumb asses up! That's the greedy muthafucker. He only wants to feed himself! I handed this business over to you and you failed me! I trusted you to keep me out the streets! I've been able to lay low for the last twenty fucking years! I built this shit and trained you well, so I wouldn't have to! Now I have to come out of retirement and handle this shit!" Ole G was talking low, mad as fuck!

Sweets was feeling real stupid. "Shit, what's the plan? If I get out of here I can take care of everything!"

"No, you're going to stay put so you don't get caught up in another damn thing! Let Swift get out and handle his business! He'll take care of his problematic Moose and then we will work on getting your ass out of here! Behave yourself; I don't want any more heat coming your way! Sweets, you are now responsible for Swift. That nigga better not get one damn scratch! He's a prized possession at this point! I'll see you in a couple of weeks!" Ole G got up and walked out the visitor's room.

*****

As the CO was walking me back to the dorms I saw C-lo, who was on the same side that Swift was on, so I stopped and hollered at him real quick. Told him that all bets were off, meaning let Swift live. I was talking in code and told him to set up a meet between me and Swift. *We have to talk and set up some kind of strategy.*

I'll get to Rock in a little bit to let him know. He's still shifty about Swift killing Tiz, so I'm not sure how that's going to go! If Rock ain't talking right then he can just be eliminated. *The last thing I need is for something to happen to Swift, then that's my ass!* Whatever Ole G says do, then that's what you better do, if you want to breathe. Nobody has ever been able to shake me but him!

I was nine-years-old when he started showing me the ropes, took me under his wing, and he always told me that one day he would hand me over the business. I saw a lot of people try and cross him; no one has ever survived. After a while he never got his hands dirty. All he did was give his people the look, never opening up his mouth, and they knew that it was time to kill. Mentioning his name has got me out a lot of shit, especially with the local police. As soon as I say Ole G, they let me go. Every now and then you get a stupid rookie that don't know no better, but they catch on fast and follow suit just like the rest! From the Governor to the Mayor on down, Ole G has a reputation that don't nobody touches! *I don't know why he doesn't just have Moose smoked off instead of waiting for Swift.*

When Ole G says something you don't ask any questions, you just let him do things his way! I've seen his temper roar louder than a lion in the quietest way. You have to be there to witness it. Execution style that you never even see coming! He is the definition of Money, Power, and Respect!

*****

Swift was in line waiting to use the phone to call Diamond when C-lo approached him to let him know that Sweets wanted to have a meeting.

"I hear you C-lo, but for real, I really don't have anything to say to old dude. Now run back and tell that!" He better get the fuck out my face with that bitch shit! Like I'm stupid, nigga trying to set me up! Since when does Sweets want to talk! Huh, I am not the one! Good finally my time to get on the phone and talk to my baby.

*****

"Hey baby, what's going on?" It's always a good thing to hear Diamond's voice. Talking to her makes my days in here go a little better, even if it is only for fifteen minutes.

"Hey Babe, I'm waiting on the lawyer to call me, he's supposed to be getting a bail hearing for you." I let out a sigh of relief. Before I knew it, I was grinning from ear to ear. I had to straighten up my face. In here you can't let on to any good news. These niggas will get jealous real quick and before you know it, here comes another charge. You have to stay close lipped. *I'm not telling no one about my bail hearing.*

"Oh yeah? Just what I needed to hear. Whew, man that's what's up! Did he say what the wait time would be?" I'm trying to see how much longer I'm going to be up in this piece. *Even more of a reason to stay away from Sweets. I have to duck his ass out!*

"He said it shouldn't be long, within the next week or so! I miss my Boo!" Diamond sure nuff was proving her loyalty to me. Lala would have been creeping with the next man. Ever since she came to her senses, she's made every visit possible. I know it's only been two weeks, but in here, two weeks feels like two years!

"You already know what it is; I appreciate you and everything that you're doing for me. I know you missing NC and for you to be staying here because of me means a lot, Boo! I just want to get out of here so I can show you, not just tell you!" *Diamond deserves the world from me and she's going to get it.*

"Swift, I love you. All I want right now is you. NC may be where I want to be, but my heart is here with you. I'm not leaving you here. You need me right now, and that's all that matters to me." *Damn, it feels good to have somebody so real by my side. Down with me through the good and the bad.*

"Thanks babe, you the real MVP!" We both laughed. I turned around to be aware of my surroundings. You can never be too careful in here, even with these fake ass police. Some of them were just as corrupt as the system. All it takes is a promise, some extra dollars added on to the underpaid paycheck, and they'll sell out quick. "So what's the word on the street, you find anything out yet?" I asked Diamond to find out what was up with Moose and his lack of. I know he can't come to see me because of his record, but he could have put some money on my books or something.

"Yeah, I'll have to talk to you about that in person. Certain things can't be discussed on these phones!" My baby played that smart. That's why she's a Diamond. I wasn't even thinking about these recorded lines. They could have caught me slipping, but she got my back.

"You right. We'll talk about that when I see you! How's everybody doing?" I'm asking in code to get some kind of idea of what's going on. *Diamond is smart she can figure that out.*

"Not too good. Business is booming, but only one person is benefiting. They ain't even thinking about me. There's no loyalty anymore. As hard as I've worked and all that I did to help people. They set me up is what I'm hearing, but I'm supposed to find out more a little later, so we will see! I mean it was a takeover!" *I know Diamond is not trying to tell me that my right hand, Moose, turned on me and set me up!*

"Yeah babe, that's a serious problem!" That's all I was able to say before the recording came on to disconnect the call.

*****

I could feel my blood boiling, hands shivering, lip shaking, it just can't be! My road dawg that I put in the game, my brother from another mother, my boy that I rocked and rolled with all day, every day! He did this shit to me! He had me set up to take over territories. Nah, Diamond has to be wrong on this shit! She got something mixed up, must be a misunderstanding or she heard wrong!

I waved over to C-lo because now I need him. He can make a couple of calls to find out what's really good! If this is true, then

Moose will die a nice, slow death. It ain't going to be nothing fast like a bullet to his head. You don’t go out like that for some green with dead Presidents!

CHAPTER 7

LALA

Looking ugly every day was surely taking a toll on me. Nina suggested that I get some help. I slapped the shit out of that bitch! What the hell I look like sitting down talking to some shrink that has to be just as crazy as me? I never understood that job. All that schooling to sit down and listen to people talk to you about all of their problems. All you need is a good listening ear to do that!

I remember when my mother took me to see one, talking about I had 'daddy issues,' no I had issues with her weak ass! The so-called therapist asked me to talk about what was on my mind so I asked her was she married? When was the last time her husband fucked her real good? How good did she move her pussy? That was it, she told my mother to never bring me back to her! I laughed my ass off that day! I guess I was a bit much for her and that's exactly what I wanted!

*****

I finally let Nina eat me the other day, figuring that it would ease some of my stress. Boy was I wrong! Not even sex could take my mind off of my face! I don't know how ugly people even live. They might as well just do us all a favor and kill themselves! At least I have a little bit of hope. I have to just wait this out and see what the end results are. A couple of years is a long time, but if that's what it takes to make me beautiful again, then I can lay low until then.

I have another surgery scheduled again in six weeks and I can't wait! I sent Nina out to get me a bunch of hijabs to cover up my face, for now. I'm a fake Muslim only to go back and forth to the doctors. The rest of the time I'm either sleeping or plotting on Moose.

*****

Moose let power go straight to his head just like a dope fiend shootin up! At first everything was running nice and smooth, then I started noticing that Moose was treating me like I was his intern instead of his partner. I'm the one that came up with the plan to set up Swift, Sweets, and Rock! I was planning to do it on my own and bring Moose down right along with them, but decided against it, and put him in on the takeover. Swift would have been too hard to set-up considering the terms we were on. I needed Moose to help me with my plan.

I rolled up on the Alameda, tooted my horn, and signaled for him to get in the car. Lucky for me it didn't take too much to persuade Moose to see things my way. He's always been about them dollars anyway, so once I started putting numbers out there and convinced him that Swift has always been using him in the first place, he wanted in! The lies just flowed out of my mouth. Telling him how Swift was jealous of him, how Swift wanted him out of the game so he could have all the money to himself. I told him that Swift fucked every chick he had ever been with, including Binky. That the two of them were on the low and that was the real reason why I told her probation officer on her! I cried in his arms to make the shit more believable and he fell for it! As a topping I fed him some dessert of my bodily juices! An extra payback to Swift and Binky!

Now I wish I would left that one-time deal alone! Moose had it in his head that we were going to be some kind of power couple! Oh no Boo Boo, we might have mixed a little business with pleasure, but let's not get it twisted, I don't and never have wanted him! I just used him up for that moment to get what I wanted at that time. That's what I do! I had to constantly remind Moose that it wasn't that type of party! *Niggas always want more of La!*

Swift was the only one that did me dirty! He thought he was leaving me assed out; it was only out of fairness that he would suffer and feel my wrath! I warned him on more than one occasion, now he's behind them bars! After all these years of landing in second place, playing her side chick role, the bitch lands in first place! I wonder how she's feeling right now taking collect calls, seeing her man behind bars without a chance of ever hitting the bricks! I know her pussy is aching and throbbing for some dick! Now I get to laugh. I have a score to settle with her that's been a long time coming! Right now I have to deal with Moose first, as unforeseen circumstances have let me up off her trail.

Diamond has been missing for a minute. *She must be laying low!* Hopefully she will come out of hiding before I bring her out! She's going to pay for sleeping behind me with every dude that I've been with. Her pussy is always somewhere up in the mix. Planning of my own in progress.

*****

Moose's thinking must be off; he isn't on point. Well, maybe because I didn't tell him everything. I work the East, West, South, and North. I'm known all over, and because I had a 'hands on' with Sweets' boys, I built a relationship with them. I promoted and put them in places that Sweets, Swift, and Rock never would. On top of that, I was sliding them extra money in the pockets, so happy with me they are! My mind always has the 'what if' factor going on. There's always a method to my strategies. So, if this day should ever come, I knew I had back up! Their trust lies within me now. I could have Moose taken out, like yesterday, but I have better for him! Since money is his pleasure I need to watch him lose everything, and I won't be happy until he's living like a homeless man! He needs to be stripped, begging for a penny! He ruined my face; the one thing that got me through this hell of a life we live in, and I'm going to make sure that he pays very dearly! Once I accomplish that, then he can die!

*****

"Hey Sweetie!" I hear Nina calling me. She's getting too used to using her key so freely. Coming in and out of here like she got it like that! I gave her that key for emergency purposes only! Nina found me in the bedroom lounging around as usual.

"Hey, how did it go?" I asked Nina to go meet Moose to pick up my money from over East. Nina threw me my black bag.

"It went okay. You know I can't stand that motherfucker! He had the nerve to ask me 'did you say anything about who shot you yet?' I'm doing what you told me to do, but the shit is hard! I don't understand why you won't just turn him in! Do you know how much time he can get for shooting you? It's so easy to do that! I could have just put a few bullets in him myself! What's the hold up?" Nina has been anxious to get ahold of Moose ever since I told her. I'm starting to regret telling her. She's going to fuck shit up for me!

"I need to do this my way! I've been doing a lot of working from home and I don't need you messing this up! Moose will come crashing down. My plan starts tonight! If I have him locked up he will expose this whole operation and we all go down! I'm letting him roam the streets on purpose!" My guys are in motion to rob one of his houses tonight and take all of his stash. I would have them set the bitch on fire, but I already pulled that stunt on Swift, so it would be obvious. I want to leave him wondering.

"Okay, do it your way! I wish you would let me in on the plan. Since when do we keep stuff from one another? I really love you La, anybody that hurts you, hurts me! You got me out here playing nice with the scum! I'm being phony as fuck. Phony ain't never been in my bones! The shit I do for you!" Nina shook her head as she was sitting down next to me on the bed.

"Nina, listen to me, in this life that we are living you're going to have to be phony sometimes to get what you need! You're on the front line now, not behind the scenes. Just looking pretty ain't gonna cut it. The shit we do is ugly!" Nina struck a nerve with me. She's too used to being with Sweets and not really having to do nothing but follow his lead. She has to get out of that, especially with me being under the radar. I'm depending on her to do what I can't do.

"Sweets wasn't phony. If he didn't fuck with you, then you knew it, and that was that! With him it was cut and dry! If he even thought that you fucked him over, it was bye, bye; you would never see them again! You had him fooled. I was always in his ear about you! He didn't listen and look where he's at now. But that was before me and you started hooking up. You're so good La, that even I wonder sometimes if I'm just a game to you, or if you really care about me. Lately I've been questioning myself!" *Now here she goes with this bullshit!* If I didn't have a need for Nina she wouldn't be around me, just like that! *These are the most ungrateful people that I put on! She has more money than she ever had in her life. Sweets only gave her what he wanted her to have. Here I have set her up with the good life and she's questioning me!*

"Nina get out your feelings, you're upset and feeling some kind of way because I won't let you fuck me! That's all this is about!" If I were to cock my legs open and let her strap on then I wouldn't even be hearing this shit!

"That's not what this is about. Sex is a small thing! I can find somebody to run up in between my legs and lick me down! What worries me the most is if you're trying to set me up! Trust is coming into play now! I show you loyalty; do you show me? No, you don't! I don't know what angle you're coming from!" That's the point. She's not supposed to know where I'm coming from. That's where people mess up…when they're so predictable.

"Nina, please, I'm going through a lot right now and the last thing I need is for your mind to be drifting. I care about you and would never let anything happen to you! Where would I benefit from setting you up?" *If Nina really knew me then she would know that I never do anything that's not beneficial to me. I'm selfish like that.*

"I don't want to be your crutch Lala. I want to be the woman that you love and need! I think I have the answer that I needed." Nina got up and grabbed her keys. This is what she does when she gets mad at me lately. *Just leave already!* "Oh by the way, Moose wants to talk to you. He's growing impatient! You might want to pick up your phone the next time he calls! I'm taking a few days off from you. There's enough food in the fridge and take out menus in the drawer!"

I waited until I heard the door shut before picking up the phone and calling Moose. Now that the plan was set in place, I think I can stand to hear his voice.

*****

"It's about damn time!" Moose picked up the phone. No 'Hello, how are you?'

"What do you want?" I asked, as my stomach was getting nauseous from the sound of his voice.

"Well damn, I was just calling to check on you! I see you didn't tell nobody nothing! How's the face coming along anyway?" Moose said laughing like shit was funny. "I told you before we even got started in this business not to cross me! Bet you won't do that no more!"

"First off, I never crossed your bitch ass! I made a deal to help somebody else out and make a few extra dollars in the process! It was a solo venture because I can! You didn't even give me a chance to explain before you shot me in the face! Our deal was our deal, and my side businesses were not included in the package!" *This nigga must have forgotten who put this whole deal together in the first place. If it wasn't for me he would still be sucking Swift's dick.*

"Nah, you said all or nothing! You can't make side deals that I don't know about. It affects business on all accounts! But you talking through this phone like you big shit! When you coming out of hiding?" *As soon as my face gets right, motherfucker. By that time your ass will be long gone away from here!*

"I'm not in hiding, I'm healing! Let's not put a rush on it. Do I sense some urgency in your voice? Now you need me! I guess you shot me a little too soon!" *Come on Moose...if I come out, your days on earth become a whole lot shorter. Don't try me!*

"Whatever you say. I'm going to be gone for a couple of weeks! I'm going on vacation to do some soul searching, so I need your flunky to take over and handle everything on her own. We are straight for a couple of days, but the guys are going to need to be working! She needs to make sure that the crew is supplied and money is collected. I'm not taking no shorts. My shit better be right too, unless she wants to look like you!" *Now he's threatening Nina. This fool really thinks this is a one man show.*

"Since when do you go on vacation? I've never known you to leave the city!" Moose was up to something, but whatever it was, was good for me because I had two weeks to cause a tornado to his life. *If he could only see the smile that was on the other end of this phone!*

"I'm leaving tonight and that's all you need to know! Have your flunky ready and give her a heads up! She won't have time to be eating your pussy and digging up your ass!" Moose hung up the phone. *I wonder how he knew what was going on between me and Nina. Nobody knew. All they knew was that she was my homegirl! NINA, YOU'RE IN FOR IT!*

CHAPTER 8

BINKY

So far L.A. is doing it for me. I'm so glad that I made the decision to move here. Life is so much different. The grass really can be greener on the other side. I haven't had the chance to see what the hood looks like yet. I know they have one, every major city does. Not in a rush either. Seen the hood all my life, but just a little curious to see what it's all about.

*****

I had that little misunderstanding with Jay, trying to convince her that keeping the money that I stole from Moose would benefit us both. She wasn't trying to hear it! Jay has been gone too long. I don't think she thought the whole thing through thoroughly; she just straight went into panic mode. I'm damned if I do and damned if I don't. The way Moose carries it, is even if I were to bring him back his money there's still consequences for stealing it in the first place. Moose would try to kill me either way. There isn't an out for me. Even if he comes hunting for me, it will be a long time before he even gets to me. I could be anywhere in L.A., and knowing Moose, he'll be too scared of losing money back home.

I even posted a picture of me, supposedly in Miami Beach, on all my social media sites. When Jay called questioning me about it, I told her that was the fake-out, to throw Moose off. To buy me some time to put that money back in the house. She thinks I went back to B-more to return the money, but like I said, he ain't getting shit back!

I rented me a hotel room and stayed there for a whole week, with some company of course. Me and Freddy been staying in touch all of this time, so he knew that I was coming. We managed to sneak out of the hotel a few times without me getting caught by Jay. Now that I know her schedule, I could have been out and about the whole time and she would have never caught me. I hate lying to my girl, but what she was asking me to do was so unreasonable. The only way I would be able to stay with her, the kids and Grams, was to make her think that I gave that money back. I did have enough to just branch out on my own, but I'm so used to living with somebody that the thought scared me to death.

*****

I admire Jay for all that she does for those kids. Most women would have kicked them to the curb once the relationship was over. Boss and Tasha could care less about their children. I haven't even seen Boss come through to check on them, and I've been here two weeks, going on three. All respect lost for them. They turned my girl into a mother before she even had a chance to give birth to her own. Jay, with the help of Grams has taken on full responsibility of them kids. It's a challenge dealing with the different attitudes and temper tantrums. This one wants this and that one wants that. Kids really are a full-time job. I just hope she don't get burned out when it comes time for her to have her own.

*****

I've always wanted my own family, seeing that I've never had any besides my Uncle. My babies will have mommy with or without daddy. They won't have to live with pain every day, nor do half the things I had to do. Walking around, only imagining who mommy and daddy are.

I'm going to assume that they're both just dead. Somebody would have come knocking by now, looking for me. When I came home from jail I asked my Uncle one last time, 'Who were my parents?' 'Where is the rest of our family?' All he did was go back in the room, shut his door and ignore me. Something that he does every time I lash out! It's crazy when you don't know who gave you life! Now I'm at the point where if it's meant for me to know, then it will come out to surface.

*****

Freddy and I have discussed raising a family together, and he feels the same way I do. If things work out, or not, we both agreed to be a part of our children's lives. He grew up without his father, watching his mother struggle just like the rest of the world. Judging by what I know, you either follow in your father's footsteps, or you step up and be the father that he never was. Men can say what they want, but the only way to tell, sho nuff, is once that bundle of responsibility arrives. I'm pessimistic; that's all my eyes have seen until proven different. That way I can never be let down because I never thought more anyway.

Fred does have a situation going on with his 'so-called' girl. Some chick named Monica that he met while I was locked up. A man is going to be a man, it's not like I had any stakes on him. He was able to stay with me that week because of his hype-man duties. He could always be out of town at any given moment. I respect his honesty. Niggas lie, and I consider him to be that one percent that tells the truth. She's a mother of two, but neither child belongs to him. For now, I'm playing the role of the long lost cousin from B-more. She seems to be cool. I did her hair the other day, impressed her with my skills of course. It was nothing special, just a bang wrap that I sewed in with that Baltimore touch. I would rock with her if I wasn't fucking her man.

With the way Monica moves and the people that she's connected to, I need her in my corner right now. Because of her, I'm already building clientele. She owns a boutique. When her customers come in and compliment her hair, she refers them to me. *That right there has been helping me and Jay.* I'm ready to go all in and open up shop, but I have to continue to play broke.

*****

I signed myself up for school to obtain my license in cosmetology. I did it for Jay. Truth be told, I don't want to see no more school. It was hard enough getting a diploma; still don't know how that happened. I was barely in class, never did any of the homework and stayed suspended. When I walked across that stage, that was it for me. I don't need no license to create beauty. I'm going to let my skills take me to the top. I can teach the shit myself! More than likely I can teach the teacher.

*****

Well, Fred just texted me that he's outside. We're still getting to know each other, so he will be sitting for a few. He has to learn that if he says four o'clock, that Bink will be ready by six. I'm never on time, unless it's for a client. *At least I have my clothes on. I just need to put this hair up in a nice little bun, throw my shoes on and I'm out.*

*****

"Aunt Binky, are you going out with that guy again?" Shayla asked, twirling around in a circle smiling.

"Yes I am. How did you know?" I asked smiling back. *Kids notice everything.*

"Because you've been in the mirror and changed like five times. I was counting, and you only do that when he's coming. Why can't he just come in here and y'all stay with us? I don't like when he takes you away. I won't see you until tomorrow." *Aww she melts my heart. I see now that kids get attached very easily.*

"Well I don't really want to introduce you to him until I see if this going to be a permanent thing. That's why you haven't met him yet. I'm not staying out late tonight. I'm going to make sure that I'm back here before you go to bed tonight. Is that okay with you, Missy?" I asked as I was putting the last pin in my hair.

"Yay! I'm going to be up too!" *This child was a mess.* I gave her a kiss and ran out the door because Fred was blowing up my phone.

*****

"Hey." I jumped into his car.

"Yo, what took you so long? I told you four o'clock, yo!" Fred said sounding impatient and irritated with me. I'm used to it, that's always the case.

"Sorry babe," I leaned over and gave him a kiss on the cheek. "The kids were holding me up." I lied just a little bit. *I can see I'm going to have to whip Fred into Binky's world. He needs to be able to time me out.*

"You lucky you fine, if you was some ugly chick I would have pulled off!" Fred laughed at his own joke. From the looks of Monica and me he didn't fuck with no ugly chicks, so that would never happen. Reading in between the lines, another way of saying he's glad that he waited for me, and I'm looking about just right. *Amazing what a sundress and sandals can do for a man.*

"Umhmmm. I guess that's a compliment! I'll take it. So where are we going today?" Every day Fred has been coming to get me, taking me out around town. I'm starting to learn my way around.

"I don't know. Do you have any place in mind?" he asked.

"I would like to see the hood around these parts." I said with excitement in my voice. You would think that I was tired, but that's all I know. I'm out of my element. It won't hurt me to know where it's at.

"Really Bink? What the fuck? Are you homesick already? Okay, I'm only doing this for you, because I stay far away from anybody's hood. Trust me, I don't want no reminders! Crips and Bloods run deep. Certain areas you don't even go in if you're not one of them. I will take you to my old neighborhood. We'll be safe over there." Fred was sounding a little scared. I'm used to dealing with niggas that will bust a cap in that ass at the drop of a dime.

"That's what I meant, show me where you came from baby! I want to know everything about you!" I'm just boosting up his ego and changing his mood. He could have taken me to any hood and I would have been fine. I can handle myself, let me find out that I'm dealing with a punk.

CHAPTER 9

CHESAPEAKE DETENTION CENTER

"I set up this meeting to get some shit straight! Now none of us are doing each other any good by being on opposite sides. We ain't got to be friends, but we need to work together so we all can get the fuck out of here! Are y'all with me?" Sweets asked me and Rock. But this overly crazed dude, Rock, is looking at me like he wants to do something. I got both my eyes glaring at him and I ain't taking them off of him.

"I don't trust this fool, Sweets!" Rock was pointing at me.

"Man, put that shit to the side. Bottom line is, ain't none of us making any money and niggas is out there playing the shit out of us. Nobody, and I mean nobody, is putting money on my books except for an Ole G! You over here talking about trust. Where the fuck is your crew and what are they doing for you? Whenever I try to call my boys they're unreachable, and we ain't getting no visits. Which means, they have turned on us! None of them niggas was loyal to any one of us! We got set up by Moose and he's Swift's problem! A debt needs to be settled!" Now they both were looking at me, but I'm trying to figure out where this convo is going.

"What are you trying to say?" Rock was just as lost as me.

"I'm saying that Swift needs to get out and handle his business! If we play our cards right then we all can see the light of day!" Sweets punched the table that we were sitting at, making our spot hot. Now the guards are looking in our direction ready to face off.

"Man, we don't need no attention drawn over here at us!" I said.

"Yes we do, they know we don't get along and have been at each other's throats! What we don't want to do is state the obvious." *Okay Sweets got one up on me with that bullshit.*

"Sweets, we got caught in a fucking warehouse with kilos of drugs, we ain't getting off on this shit man! Face the fact that this is our new home until we get sentenced and they ship us off to wherever!" Rock just wasn't getting where Sweets was going, but I understand clearly.

"Listen Rock, I know what it looks like. Don't let them prosecutors get in your head! I got a plan that will set us free! I'll put it to you this way, I meet with my lawyer tomorrow. We're taking this to trial. Yes, we're guilty, but the Feds didn't follow protocol either. We can get off, but it's going to take some time." *Sweet's isn't lying, my lawyer was digging deep to find something corrupt.*

"Well I don't have a lawyer. They appointed me to a death sentence, that's my definition of a public defender! All my money is in the streets. I have nobody to pay for me a lawyer!" *I can't believe that Rock was just this damn stupid! You mean to tell me he don't have no money put up for times likes this. It's not like we were out there nickel and diming. We were getting that money. Nigga can't be broke!* Sweets was looking at him like he had ten heads and my eyes never left the sight of him.

"Bullshit, we make too much money for you not to have none! Stop being cheap with your life and hire a fucking lawyer!" Sweets wasn't buying it and neither was I.

"I'm for real. I make it, spend it, and re-up! I was taking care of my entire family. I was paying mortgages, rent, car payments, all household bills, insurance, groceries, plus meeting wants!" *This idiot was all street minded and not business minded. His money was coming in and going out just that fast. Yep he's broke! As far as I'm concerned, he can stay in here. Me and Sweets can put it all on him. I'd rather take a lesser charge anyway.*

"Alright listen, since your stupid ass was doing all of that. I'm offering to pay for your lawyer! You have my word!" Sweets beat his chest. "You owe me, though! I want all my money back! I'm going to have Ole G set everything up for you!" Sweets was better than me. I wouldn't do shit for him. Rock played the game all kinds of stupid; he wasn't worried about times like this. Anytime you're in this game this type of shit happens. It ain't his first time! I remember when we are on the come up, I used to get caught up all the time. Nothing ever stuck, but I saw him in there a few times when I was down.

"Alright then, let's talk!" Now he's interested. Nigga is blowing my mind right now! *Chow time is almost up, so they better make this quick!*

"Moose planned a takeover and he succeeded, so he thinks! Let's clear Swift; he didn't know what he was bringing to us! We take the fall!" Sweets pointed to himself and Rock. "We need him out to handle Moose. In the meantime, we take this thing to trial! But Swift, you can't fuck us. If you do, then your ass is as good as dead! While we're in here we want our money to be stocked up! We also want to be taken care of."

"Fuck no! You're asking me to trust this cat right here! I'll sell out before I do some shit like this! It's a known fact that he killed Tiz! It's a known fact that Moose is like a brother to him. You think he's really going to kill him? Swift don't have the heart, he's to vested in that nigga! Me or you need to get out of here and handle Moose because we don't give a flying fuck! He's going to get out and say the hell with us!" *Oh here we go with this again. 'He killed my cousin.' Rock better take this deal or else!*

"See, now you're beginning to piss me off! No brother of mine would have set me up! Moose did this shit to all of us and it may not be personal to y'all, but it is to me! The day I get out of here, in less than a week, the nigga will be a has been! This hurt me to my heart! I'm going to handle mine. I could get out of here in fifteen years and I'll still make him bleed! It's to the point that if another motherfucker takes Moose's life before I get the chance to do it, then they cancel their life and their whole family! He fucked up the brotherhood when he decided to be greedy! I kept wondering why he wasn't in that warehouse! Moose was supposed to be in there and in here with us! I thought he was behind me, and the snitch never made it in! It's not an accident, and he will be dealt with accordingly! Now Rock, since you want to talk about facts, it's a known fact that you don't like me and I don't like you, but I've never been labeled as a sell-out! I'm a man of my word. Always have been! Now if I make a pact to do something then I'm going to follow through! Maybe you like it in here, but I don't! If me and Sweets is on the same page, what do you think we can do to you? We can fry your ass, but I'm not trying to go that route. We all was out here gettin money with no problems! You stayed in your lane and I stayed in mine! There was a certain level of respect that we had for one another! Yes, you lost a cousin and not too long after that I lost Jock! You left his head on my car, man. Do you hear me bringing that up in your face every five seconds? You took a life from me!" *They may have thought that I forgot about my boy, hell naw! Jock lives within me everyday. Another unsolved situation that I have to take care of.*

"I didn't have anything to do with Jock! If you know me then you'll know that I always go after the culprit! That's not my motto! I was coming straight after you! You were in the club that night and fired off them shots! The problem is we both took a loss, but yours didn't come from me! That same shit you just ran to me, I need to run back to you! I will never be satisfied until I kill your ass!" *My gut is telling me that Rock is telling the truth. If he didn't have anything to do with Jock's murder, then who did? Was it Sweets?*

"Okay fellas, we're getting off track now. Y'all beef has nothing to do with us getting out of here! Keep that shit separate! If you keep dwelling on that then it's back to square one! Wrap this right here around both of y'all small brains, can't nobody kill nobody if it's not their time! I know what I did out here in these streets, but I come from a spiritual background. I just chose a different path. Don't think that I'm up in here just reading the Bible because I'm in here. I read the Bible every night before I closed my eyes when I was out there on the bricks! I believe in a higher power and ain't no way you die before your time! When God says so, that's when you go! Look at Johnny, he got shot twenty times, but he's in here with us!" Sweets pointed at Johnny sitting at the other table. "Shot in the head two times, so all this revenge and get even shit is nonsense. Rock, you can do whatever you want to Swift, but if the good Lord don't want his chapter to end, it's not!" *Now Sweets wants to be a preacher and take us to church.*

*****

Meeting adjourned. Chow time was up. We all walked off back to our dorms. Hopefully we can meet again tomorrow. My bail hearing is in a couple of days; I should be getting out of here anyway. I don't want to let that out of the bag until the day it happens.

I hope like hell it don't make the news. Moose don't need no heads up! I want to catch him off-guard to see what lie he tries to come up with. It really don't matter, he's a dead man. I hope his time is up and God don't have no more use for him. Surely I don't! One thing is for sure, if he should live, he's going to wish he was dead by the time he recovers.

CHAPTER 10

NINA

Who does Lala think I am? I never said anything to Moose about our relationship. She's too busy questioning my loyalty and I don't appreciate it at all. I've been staying away from her depressed ass! Nope, she's all on her own. The only thing that I'm doing is handling the business that's expected of me.

She must be eating out again, I haven't been over there to cook a damn thing! This last week has me feeling so free. You never realize how far you're tied up in the knot until you let it loose! I was so caught up in her and her depression that I started feeling those same feelings. She was draining me dry! It's like a breath of fresh air. Of course, I still worry a little bit about her. Is she taking her meds? How's she feeling? What's on her mind? All I do is think about being her punching bag and my thoughts immediately change back to me and my happiness. I still have mad love for her, but I have to take care of me.

Lala only calls me when it comes to business or if she needs me to do something for her. Other than that, she don't ring my phone. *Until I become a priority in her life then I will continue to carry it the way I am.* For too long I have let my world revolve around hers. Everything had to be her way; when and what she wanted to eat, when and how she wanted to have sex, when and where she wanted to go! I'm sick and tired of meeting her needs while mine get thrown by the wayside.

My to-do list was complete. *Today, I'm doing me.* I'm going to get some much needed retail therapy done. Might just take a nice ride to Tyson's Corner. Then go to the spa and pamper myself. After that go get me some drinks. *I'm in the mood for some mingling with some familiar faces. Oh lord, now this depressed bitch is calling me.* I shouldn't answer; just let her get the voice mail. She's not fucking up my flow today. I don't care what's going on, she will just have to do it. Nina is closed for business today. It's nice out, the sun is shining and I'm in a great mood. *Let me answer this and get it over with!*

*****

"Yes, how can I help you?" Since we're keeping it strictly business, this is how I've been answering the phone.

"Hey, just wanted you to know that everything that I set in place for Moose has been in motion." La was making it seem like I was a part of her plan. *She didn't tell me shit so what the fuck is she talking about?*

"What's in motion? As far as know, I wasn't a part of anything!" *I hope she doesn't think that this would impress me.*

"I know, but I do understand that it's been bothering you, and baby, I told you I had it all under control. All you had to do was be a little bit patient with me." Today La wants to be nice to me all of a sudden. She's just leaving out one huge detail…the problem is not Moose!

"I ran out of patience when you decided to question my loyalty! Where was I since the day Moose shot you? Who took care of you? Who did everything that you asked of me?" It's my turn to go into bitch mode.

"Listen babe, just come on over here. I been missing you and I know you miss me. You will be happy to know that I've been taking my medicine, even fed myself a few times." *Did she just say come over? Did she not even apologize for all the hell she took me through? Naw boo, you coming at me wrong! It's an epic fail!*

"Sorry, my day is already planned out! Maybe another time, and not on your time! I'll let you know when I'm available." There was a time when I would drop everything to be with Lala. After putting up with her abusive ways, I'm at the end of the rode. She has to be the one to turn things around, that's if I even want her. This time by myself was a bad mistake for her. If you leave anyone alone long enough they will get to see what they're truly not missing.

"What the fuck you mean, you got plans? Since when do you pass up a chance to sniff up my ass? Who are you licking on Nina?" La kind of sounded a little thrown off by my statement. That's a narcissist for you; if it ain't about her then it really doesn't matter. I see her confidence was back on a thousand.

"Well, when I was there you didn't want me there! I gave you what you wanted and removed myself. Deal with it!" I lashed back at her, words that she would always say to me.

"I'm over here living in hell and you're talking to me like this! I haven't been outside in months, locked up in this condo like I'm in prison. Feeling depressed day in and day out, not able to look at myself, and all you're worried about is yourself! Today is the first day that I've felt good in a very long time. Finally, I made my moves on Moose and it feels so good! I wanted you take me out, drive me around for a while. I want to check on the neighborhoods since that ugly mothafucker is gone!" *Oh now she wants to go out. I been trying to get her to get some fresh air.*

"You don't miss me. You called me to use me! Take your car. You can drive, and put that thing over your head! You can handle it!" I hung up the phone.

*****

Lala was ringing my phone back to back like I was going to answer. *I'll answer when I feel like it.* What I find so funny is the fact that she still thinks she's running things. She thinks that I don't know about her having Moose's houses robbed. All his stash was gone and sitting right here in my apartment. I did split a good amount with the boys. I'm running shit now. That's what happens when you can't handle your own business. All they see is me and not her, so of course, I assumed the position; especially after she told all the head men in charge to answer to me. Lala can't call the shots without it going through me first. I'll let her think that she's still in charge, until she gets it twisted. For now I'll continue on with my beautiful day.

*****

Instead of going all the way to Tyson's Corner, I settled for Arundel Mills and shopped my ass off. Four hours in the mall, going in and out of stores. I must have bought me a whole new wardrobe. Clothes galore, shoes for days, a couple of *Michael Kors* pocketbooks, some new jewelry…*I'm all set.* A couple of trips back to the car, loading up bags, and thinking of Sweets and the shopping sprees that he used to send me on.

Lately I've been doubting my decision to help Lala with that set-up. She had a way of talking people into some mess. During my travels today I'm going to put some money on his books and write him a letter. Just to see how he's holding up.

I've been keeping a close eye on the case that the Feds were building up and looks like he's going to be in there for a very long time. He'll be an old man before he ever gets out. *The man did take care of me for years.* We had that Bonnie and Clyde foundation before Lala came into the picture. You know that saying, 'If it ain't broke, don't fix it'…I totally went against the green, stupid me. My little soft spot for the women overruled good dick anyday! That's why Sweets couldn't get enough of me. He always had treats because that's what I liked. Offer a nigga heaven and you always get some act right.

At first I think Lala's intentions were to try and scoop up Sweets away from me, but he never strayed, and had no intentions on leaving his prized possession. Why would he? I don't think it took her long to figure that part out. You can only become a competitor if you bringing some competition. Lala was too selfish, not wanting to share. I've never been the overly jealous type, just be honest with me. That's something that Lala has a problem doing. Old Leroy, her so-called trainer, the man that she's getting dick from, that she thinks I don't know about. The one thing you don't want to do with me is play me for a fool.

Leroy was ringing her phone after hours and La would all of sudden have to use the bathroom. Depending on the conversation, she would start an argument to try and get me to leave. Those are the nights that I knew he would be coming over to hit that. All she had to do was ask me to join in, no need for the secrets. Since she decided that's how she wanted to do things, it was only fair that I repay her with some secrets of my own.

*****

Well she's right, I have been kicking it lately with this dude named, Terrance. He definitely was uplifting, compared to being torn down by La. He's becoming attached to me. Supposedly, he has a girl or baby mama but I can't tell. He's been glued to my pussy day in and day out.

He took me to meet his mother. She seems to be a pretty cool lady. We had a nice conversation about Terrance; she said she's very overprotective of her baby. I understand, I would be too if I was a mother.

We have a date tonight. I plan on making it epic. Might even see if we can pick us up a treat that will leave the club with us. If not, I can always make a couple of phone calls. I'm a sucker when it comes down to a woman groaning and moaning. I get all hot and bothered when I watch a man going in and out of a pussy! *Yes baby, it's on tonight. Looking forward to it, in more ways than one.*

CHAPTER 11

JAY

I can't believe that Boss had the nerve to come over here trying to use the kids to threaten me to get some money out of me. He said he was taking them from me if I didn't give him a thousand dollars. I laughed so hard that my ribs were hurting! High out his mind on God knows what this time! *What did he think, that I was going to pay him to take care of his kids?* He reminded me of the reason why I prefer just to drink, maybe smoke some weed here and there and never to do anything stronger than that. His brain went missing, coming in here with that mess!

For some dumb reason I actually thought he was really just coming to see his kids, maybe spend some time that was needed with their father. I opened up the door with no precaution once I heard his voice. A bad, bad mistake. Had I listened closely, I would have heard his slurred speech. The excitement from his kids screaming, 'Daddy, Daddy,' had me overjoyed from the smiles across their faces. That quickly disappeared once he came through the door.

Boss barely even spoke to them. All he wanted to do was harass and try to taunt me. I asked him to leave three times, in a very nice way. By the third time he had grabbed me by my throat. The kids started screaming and kicking him. That's when Binky came flying out of the shower, not really knowing what the fuck was going on, towel wrapped around her, soap still on her body. We all went to work on that ass, including Grams. She threw a water bottle; hit Boss right in the face too. Grams throw shot was always on point. She got me a few times when I would get out of hand. Every now and then I would get to running off with a case of the smart mouth and she would knock me right back to reality. *Now was not the time for his shenanigans.*

It took us over two hours trying to calm the kids down. They were tore up; crying, and just so upset! *I can't allow them to go through that again!* For any child to have to turn on their own father is devastating. The last thing I want for them is to grow up hating him. Here I had to go again trying to explain to them that, 'Daddy is sick right now, when he gets better he will be back to normal.' After a while the story gets old. My words were becoming redundant to them. *What else can I say? I feel like somebody just took a knife and cut me in the heart with it.*

*****

"Jay, we have to do something about him!" Binky was pissed.

"Like what? He needs to get some help!" *I'm just so torn right now.*

"Yeah well, I'm ready to help him! These kids don't need this shit in their life. We need to move and you need to change their school. You heard how he was threatening to take them!" *Whew what a relief. I thought Bink was going to say something about trying to kill him.*

"We can't up and move them again. Plus, we don't have money like that!" Binky always thinks things are just so easy to do when it's not. Plus, they like the schools they go to. Kids have a hard time with change. It's not like we're in the military, hopping around from place to place. So far I have been able to provide them with stability, and will continue to do so.

"I can borrow the money from Fred and we can be gone! What are you going to do, wait until it's too late? You don't have legal custody. He's the father, he can come take them and ain't shit you can do about it. Then what?" *My mind is all over the place. Bink is right. I don't have a leg to stand on. As if I want to hear that right now.*

"I'm going to get him to sign something, even if I do have to pay him!" Unfortunately, Boss can be bought. *He'll do anything to get high.*

"We can't send them to school on Monday, that's all he's waiting for!" Binky's paranoimia was setting in. If Boss wanted to take the kids he would have. He's sleeping on the streets himself.

"They're old enough to call me if he tries anything stupid! They won't go with him anyway. I'm just going to explain the situation to the school. I have a good rapport with them anyway. What I need to do is find Tasha. Shit is out of hand!" Binky rolled her eyes at me.

"What's that supposed to do? Please tell me! The woman hasn't even checked on these kids! Jay, you know I'm extra sensitive when it comes down to stuff like this! I don't know what's worse, not ever knowing your parents or knowing and feeling like they don't want you! I think I'm better off. I hate to see kids hurting over fucked up ass parents. They didn't ask for this shit!" As I watch the tears roll down Binky's face I can see just how much this is really bothering her.

"I need to take a ride. I'll be back." I said as I was grabbing my keys to walk out the door.

*****

I couldn't sit in there any longer looking at a bunch of sad faces. Grams locked herself in her room, the kids were in their room and Binky was on the couch crying. *Today has been a very upsetting day.*

Boss needs to figure out what he's going to do pertaining to these kids, and I need to file for legal custody. Bink is right. As it stands now, him or Tasha can come take them at any given moment. It's time for me to do this the right way for the safety of the children. If Boss or Tasha ever get it together, they won't get a fight from me.

All children deserve to be raised by a parent. As good as I am to them, and all that I provide, will never fill the emptiness that will be left inside of them. With both my parents getting killed, I know exactly what Binky is saying and going through. I still get upset sometimes about why God took them both. Like damn, you couldn't leave one here to raise me!

*****

I'm hurting all the way around. A man that I thought loved me has once again let me down. Boss has lied, cheated, and stole. As the old folks say, 'That's the devil.' *This was supposed to be my happily ever after ending, instead it's everything but that. Now what? What does Jay do now?* I've already been doing strange things for small change because of his kids. If it were just me and Grams, I could handle my responsibilities, but when you have a family you have to do what you have to do! *Except these weren't my kids, and I'm not receiving a dime from either parent.* My life has been put on hold. *What about my dreams? Dreams of traveling the world, beating faces all over! Dreams of me and Binky owning our own shop with so much to offer! Dreams of having my own children; I can't bring another child into this mess! How do I juggle all of that and raise three children? Lala was right about some things, never get too comfortable with a nigga! I'm already feeling some kind of way, thinking about my life is only going to make it worse. It's best for me to focus on the future and not the now. But wait, what future? Here I go again feeling like I'm back in the projects with no way out!*

*****

Of course I would find Boss hanging out in Chesterfield Square on West 54th Street. I pull over and beep the horn. He's trying to ignore me. I know damn well he sees me sitting here, and I'm not in the mood for any more scenes. I roll down the window and wave for Boss to come here and he's still ignoring me. His druggy friend is tapping him on the shoulder as Boss turns his head and begins to walk away. I don't want to play these games with him, but we have to talk and the time is now! I drive down a little and beep the horn again.

*****

"Boss, I'm not up for your shenanigans. Get in, now!" I yelled from the top of my lungs. *This nigga got some nerve playing the fucking victim.* He must have known I meant business; he came and got in the car

"What? What do you want now?" Boss said it as if I asked for him to come earlier today. *Drugs will do it to ya!*

"You really hurt the kids today, Boss! Matter of fact, from now on I will address you as Teddy. You used to be a boss, but you're all washed up now! There was a point and time when you had it all. Do you remember those times? I used to run from the paparazzi, couldn't go anywhere without a bunch of women trying to get with you, and dudes throwing mix tapes your way!" I started looking around the surroundings. "You wouldn't be caught dead in this neighborhood! This is what you plan on doing with the rest of your life?"

"What do you want, Jay? You think I want to sit here and listen to this shit! Let me live my life and you live yours!" Oh I must be getting to Teddy. He was starting to show some emotions. Hold on tight buddy, because I'm not done. This is just the beginning.

"See that's the thing, I can't live my life because I'm stuck raising your kids! While you're out here deteriorating down to nothing and your wife is M. I. Fucking A! I would love to just live my life and do Jay for a change. All my damn life I was doing what pleased everybody else and never me! Then I met you, fell in love, and was living my dreams for once, and it all came crashing down on me! While you're out here getting your fix, I'm at home helping with homework, helping Grams prepare dinner, cleaning, ironing clothes and preparing for the next day to do it all over again! This isn't the life that I envisioned for us. I had us getting married, having a couple more kids, living the life that I've always imagined. We were supposed to be that power couple, and you went and fucked it all up!" I can't even cry anymore. After enough pain shit just becomes the norm.

"I'm sorry Jay, all I ask is that you give me a minute?" I've never seen Boss cry before, but now I see the tears and I can't even feel bad for him. Nor do I feel the need to console him. I'm the one that needs consoling. Where was he all the nights that I cried in the bed alone?

"It's been a long minute already. Two rehabs that you ran out of! Shit you stole that you promised to replace. Niggas blackballing me because of choices that you made! I fuck with ballers not with dope fiends, crack heads, and pill poppers! How did you let us get here? You moved me all the way from Baltimore, for this? To cheat on me and to lie to me! You let your wife drop off three kids, knowing you were fucked up, and left them on me to raise! When is enough, enough? What's your minute when you hit the dirt because you're laying in a casket? I'm not asking you to get it together for me, I'm saying do it for yourself so that you can be the father you need to be!"

"If I do this, will you be here for me?" Boss asked sounding like a little kid begging his mother.

"In what way?" I want to make sure he understands me clearly. I don't want to give him any false hope about a me and him. It's over, I'm done!

"I need you Jay, I can't do this alone!" Wrong words for him to say to me. I've had enough of people saying they need me! You know what they gave me, a big fat ass to kiss!

"I can't tell. You didn't need me when you just threatened to take the kids away from me, when you know damn well you don't even have a place for them to lay their heads! All for a thousand dollars to get high with when you use to give out thousands like it was piss! You showed your ass!" *I'm not dismissing shit like it didn't happen just because he's crying.*

"Help me Jay. Help me please! Oh, I fucked up. I got caught up with the partying! Started dealing with the wrong muthafuckers and now I'm out here! What was once for pleasure became a habit that I need. I let that shit take over me. I know I went too far today! Please take me to the hospital so I can get the help I need!" Exactly what I wanted to hear, but my hopes were low, even though I can see that this time is different. *He might actually mean it. I'll believe it once he's clean.*

"Sure, I'm not getting out of this car or signing any papers! You're a grown man and grown men do real shit!" I drove off headed to the hospital.

CHAPTER 12

SWIFT

The judge let me out on a hundred thousand dollar bond; it wasn't as bad as I thought it was going to be. *Finally out of that hellhole. At least now I can make some moves.* Feels good to be out here on the bricks. I waited until I got back from court to send word to Sweets and Rock. I know what's expected of me and I'll deliver. As soon as I get to one of my stash spots, I'll be putting money on their books. Well, I'm going to have Diamond do it. Don't need my John Hancock on nothing.

*****

Diamond informed me that Moose is on some kind of vacation. Since when did he start doing that? Some chick must finally have his ass wide open, because Moose don't go anywhere but to pick up some money and get him some pussy.

Diamond is highly pissed off with me at the moment. I had her drop me off at my lawyer's office, told her I had to take care of some business. She wanted to wait on me, but I insisted that she wait until I called her. Had to put my foot down. Getting rid of her wasn't easy; she didn't want to leave my sight. She'll move mountains for me if she could. *Exactly the reason why I have a nice little set up for her.* Today I will not be handling any business; it's all about her!

*****

One of my stash spots wasn't far from my lawyer's office. Once I saw her pull off in a rage, that's when I eased my way up the street to the parking garage. I paid Old Man John to hold my old Ford Escort and move it every now and then. He never asked any questions, just took the money and did what I asked him to do.

*****

"Hey Swift, my young man! I was starting to get worried about you. Where you been? I miss talking to you buddy!" Some days I would just come and talk to the old man for hours at a time, just to clear my head.

"Didn't I tell you to start watching the news? I got caught up in some trouble but I'm back now! It ain't nothing that I can't handle though. How you been?" I gave Old Man John a hug.

"You know I don't watch no news. It's always bad stuff; I don't want to hear no nonsense. I'm just glad you're okay!" Old Man John grabbed his cane. "Come on, you want some good old pasta?"

"Nah, I just came to check on the car. I'm planning something really nice for my girl, hope it turns out well!" I'm just ready to get to my stash. Hate to disappoint my Italian friend. I know he wants to have one of our talks, but I'll catch him at a later date.

"Oh okay, is it that Diamond?" *Oh wow, he remembers me talking about her.* Old Man John could be very forgetful at times.

"Yeah, it's her!" A man ain't supposed to get no butterflies, but I swear the minute he mentioned Diamond's name I felt something warm in my stomach.

"Good. She's special, Swift. You better be good to her! That other one you had was noooo good for a man of your caliber. I been starting her up and moving her around just like I always do! I'll sit here and wait for you. Here are the keys! She's up on level three, back in the corner." *Damn I got love for this old man. Even though he hadn't seen me in months, he still did what I asked him to do. He's more loyal to me than the niggas I fed and bred. I get locked up and they just forgot all about me. Sooner than later a dose of reality will hit them.*

*****

My old sugar was buffed up and shining. He even gave her a nice bath. She was my very first car and I kept her. Everybody needs a reminder of just how far they came every now and then. You won't catch me riding in her down the street, but I have no problem taking her for a spin in the garage. I started her up; she sounded good as new, pulled down my back seat car cover and lifted up the seat, and there sat my stash. I counted up ten g's. *That should be enough for today.* Running around with a bunch of money on me was always a 'no no' in my book. Satisfied, I drove down to the first floor and parked my sugar in the parking spot next to Old Man John's office. As I got out the car I had to do a double take.

"Man oh man, you really did the damn thing! She ain't never been buffed up like that! How much I owe you?"

"Nothing. You overpaid the last time, but I'm glad you like! I was in here bored with nothing to do and decided to make her my project. I impressed myself actually. An old man like me still got it!" Very rarely have I ever seen Old Man John smile, but this was twice in one day.

"Alright, I'll be back sometime this week to check you out!" I rolled out; thought about catching a hack for a second. Not a good idea with the amount of money I had on me. Not to mention I wasn't strapped. I decided to take my chances in a yellow cab. I was only a couple blocks away from the train station, so feet don't fail me now. I knew there would be plenty in the waiting.

*****

This was the longest two blocks that I ever walked. I was trying to stay on the low. Saw a couple of little hustlers that worked for me. Just wondering why they were over this way and not up by Greenmount Ave. I managed to sneak on by them without being noticed. *Good for me, bad for them because they weren't on point.* See, I didn't play that sloppy shit. You have to be aware of your surroundings at all times. If somebody wanted to rob their asses they were an easy target…or even the cops! *Not a good look, Moose. You're slipping my boy! When I start running things again they won't be getting a promotion...more like a demotion.* Once I get rid of Moose and get things up and running, I plan on leaving the business alone, but in good hands.

*****

I made the cab driver quite happy today. He ran me around, never turning off the meter. It was cool though. I got to where I needed to go and handled everything accordingly. Yeah, he was a little skeptical about me. I could tell by the way he was carrying me. While he wanted to be an ass, thinking that I was trying to beat him of his time, I made it my business to show him different. Every stop he made I had to pay him before I got out. In total, I paid him three fifty. I added a buck fifty to make it an even five hundred. He was sure to give me his phone number, telling me if I need him any time, just call! *Yeah, I bet if I was him, I would want me too!*

The Bellman at the Hyatt saw me struggling trying to get the bags out and came to my rescue. *I'm hoping they have a room available, and surely they did.* I got the key cards and arrived at the room shortly after the Bellman arrived with all my stuff that I brought from earlier. Now it was time to call Diamond and tell her where to meet me. I called three times before she answered the damn phone.

*****

"You know I don't have a phone yet. I specifically asked you to answer all unknown calls!" I already knew she was going to have an attitude from the way I brushed her off earlier.

"Yeah well, I don't listen well. All I heard was that I was not needed! I was busy packing my shit to head back to NC! You used me Swift. Got me real good this time!" Diamond was bringing on the drama and that wasn't my intention.

"I didn't use you. All I asked for was some time to handle a few things! You really think that I would dog out the only person that was there for me? Come on now Diamond, you should know me better than that. Please don't give me that charge! As much as I love you, are you for real?" Now my feelings were hurt.

"I don't know Swift. You've done it in the past! All kind of thoughts were running through my head! When a man gets out of jail, the first thing he wants is to make love to his woman. After that judge granted you bail, the first thing I did was book us a room. All you were worried about is handling business…the same thing that landed your ass in there in the first place! When am I going to be a priority?" *Shit, I should have done this different. Now Diamond is all upset, crying her eyes out! I really fucked this up!*

"Baby, can you come here so I can hold you and show you just how much you mean to me? Just hear me out one last time, then if you want to go back to NC I will have to be okay with that. Can you at least do that?" *I'm feeling like shit right about now.*

"Where is here Swift?" Diamond asked.

"I went and got us a hotel room too. At the Hyatt. I'm in room twenty-one, twenty-three." *Please Diamond, just agree to come and get that ass here.*

"Where am I supposed to park down there? You're giving me my money back from booking that room that nobody is going to be in! I'll be there in fifteen minutes!" Before I had a chance to tell her to park in the garage, she hung up on me.

I had fifteen minutes to change clothes and get my little set-up together. Looking around the room, I think I did a pretty good job for a guy who's never ever been romantic. I heard the knock on the door.

*****

"Hey you." I grabbed Diamond and slid my tongue in her mouth before I even let her in.

"Wait a minute." She pulled away from me. "Can't we do this inside and not in the hallway? That is the reason why you have a room right?" Sometimes I hate her smartass mouth.

"You right," I swung open the door. The look on Diamond's face was priceless. The room was filled with rose petals, lit candles, champagne chilling on ice, with two glasses that had *Swift* and

Diamond engraved with today's date. I added a simple touch by buying myself a nice suit; I never suit it up unless it's a funeral. Just not my style. *I hope she can fit the nice little negligee that I have laid out on the bed for her.*

"Wow! Oh my God Swift!" Diamond starting pounding me on my chest. "Why didn't you just say something? I've been upset all damn day!"

"I wanted to surprise you. Had I told you then, there would be no need. I don't want you to ever doubt my love for you! I know the past has been rocky between us, but that's just that, the past! Let's not wake up the dead! You feel me baby?" I put my arms around her from behind so we could both just stare at the art that I created and seize the moment.

"Swift, I love you!" Diamond tilted her head up looking me straight in my eyes. "This is beautiful. Did jail do this?"

"No baby, you did this! Your loyalty towards me, and love you have for me, that no other woman has ever had. I know you said your father named you, sorry he wasn't there, and missed out on the Diamond that he created." I took her by the hand and led her over to the bed so we both could sit.

"Baby, I need to be honest, when we first hooked up I really was trying to get back at Lala because of our history with dudes, but after a while, the joke was on me. I fell in love, hard for you! It was just supposed to be a game that I was playing." Diamond put her head down like she was ashamed.

"I know that, I'm not stupid! That's why I gave you a hard time. I wasn't sure if your love was genuine or not. I'm a man that wanted to hit that, that's all it was for me too at first. Then as time went on, and I saw your feelings changed into something real, that's when I let my guard down. Today is a new day and we're on a different page. All I did in there was think about you and how I was going to come out here and treat you to something special."

"You just being out is special enough for me." Diamond just cherishes the small things, such a low maintenance chick and I appreciate that in her.

"Diamond, I'm a thug. Always have been. A nine to five ain't never been my thing, but I have enough money stashed away to hold us over. Maybe even enough for the rest of our fucking lives, with your frugal ass!" She laughed at my words. "On some serious shit, I do have some stuff to handle out here for a while, but it won't be long before I get out the game. NC here I come. Once I get this court stuff out of the way, and if everything goes in my favor, I'm leaving. I'm ready for a slower pace of life, and to find something else that I like to do, besides hustling. You have been the glue that's been holding me together! I don't want this life without you, and today I would like to commit myself to you and you only. I can promise you that if you walk with me, that I'm willing to give you the world. Fuck the small talk. Will you marry me?" I pulled out a beautiful diamond ring for my Diamond.

CHAPTER 13

LALA

Where the hell is Nina? This bitch hasn't been answering her phone for the last two days, or returning any of my text messages. She's been acting real shady lately, taking advantage of my weakness. I can't stand feeling so damn vulnerable. She knows that I have surgery in the morning and she's playing games! Who the hell does she think she's fucking with? I'm the last person you want to take for a joke! She has until midnight to surface or else I'll go find her ass tonight. Moose is back, talking all stupid, accusing me of having something to do with his houses getting robbed. He's saying that it had to be an inside job and no one knew he was leaving town but me and Nina. He wants his money from the sales from the last couple of weeks, and Nina has it, not me! He didn't put in no work so I feel he shouldn't get paid. Who gets paid when they don't go to work? Nigga ain't on salary. This is street business! I may not be out there, but I'm working from home. Swift is out on bail. How in the hell did the Feds let that happen? What else could go wrong with this day? Now this bitch decides to call me!

*****

"Nina, where the hell you been? Why haven't you answered my calls or text messages? Have you forgotten who you work for?" I need some answers and this better be good.

"I was away for a couple of days, turned my phone off! I didn't want to be interrupted. Plus, everything was handled. What was the emergency anyway?" *Nina just left and didn't even tell me! Oh now I know she has lost it!*

"Are you fucking crazy? You didn't even say shit; at least Ugly gave us a heads up! Nina have you forgotten how we operate? I control this shit, your every move needs to be accounted for! I knew mixing business with pleasure was a bad idea! Please don't make me regret fucking you too! I need to see you and NOW!" *I'm gonna beat the mess out of her. Dumb ass will learn today!*

"Lala, call me back when you figure out who in the hell you're talking to! You got me all the way fucked up on every side! Last time I checked, you didn't have any kids, only that fake one you pretended to be pregnant with!" *Calm down La; think real quick, if I go off my emotions right now I'll literally kill her ass!*

"Nina, listen to me and listen nice and clearly, all hell has broken loose and you don't want this right now! Ugly is back and he wants his damn money that you have! He knows it was an inside job and is blaming me and you! One of us is the leak in his mind. Now he already shot me in the face, do you want to be next? Swift is out on bail and every minute that goes by is a minute wasted! Do you understand me? We need a plan and quickly, and my surgery is tomorrow!" *Nina needs to know that I mean business. I'm on edge and I'm not sure what I'm capable of doing to her right now!*

"Well it seems like you have some problems on your hands and none have to do with me! I do have the money for Moose, and I will gladly give it to him! As far as his houses that you had robbed, I don't know, guess you will have to figure that part out. Now Swift being out after you assured me that they would never see the light of day, that's also something you will have to figure out! Now on another note, you are no longer the head woman in charge, I am! You haven't worked these streets in months! What made you think that being in hibernation was a good idea? The guys listen to me, they pay you no mind and neither do I! Just continue to order the supplies and set-up shipments, I guess I will handle the rest and clean up your mess!" *Oh I'm over here shaking, one of us ain't gonna make it. If there's one thing I hate, it's not being in control!*

"Nina where are you?" I'm going to this bitch!

"None of your business. Now, you just do what I said and prepare yourself for your surgery. I'll come up to the hospital to see you once you're in recovery!" *No, you will see me today; little do you know! I got something for that ass. Nobody is taking over what I built. I'm getting my power back, face scarred up or not!*

"Okay Nina, have it your way! I'll see you soon!" Nina thinks she can play these kinds of games with me, like I'm some kind of toy…not today. Ain't happening! All them skills that Leroy taught me will be put into action today! Oh yeah, we gonna box today, just like they do in the ring. That's if I don't knock her ass out!

*****

Looking at myself in the mirror, the hijab has just about covered up all my scars. No matter what happens, I will be at my surgery tomorrow. The sooner I can get back to looking decent the better. The doctor said I should see a lot of improvement after this one, but it's going to take six to eight weeks for my face to heal. Nobody will recognize me.

I'm headed over to Nina's house. She thinks she can take over my life, turning my guys against me. Well Moose, she's all yours. That's why I hate fucking with bitches! They're quick to make a turn, and easy to forget who had their back! Just like Binky and Jay, turncoats. I'm tired of the bullshit and I'm not taking no more! Involving Moose and her was a terrible mistake. The good thing about Swift being out…oh he will get to Moose, I'll help him if I have to. Even though I wanted to see him suffer, I can let that go! Don't they know I'm the set-up queen? As soon as I finish fucking up Nina, I'm calling Moose to let him know that she was the one that had his houses robbed. That will take care of that problem. I see Nina's car, so she is home. Stupid, Stupid, Stupid, she thought I wasn't coming out. Poor baby! Here I come, Cunt! I'll try knocking first. If I don't get an answer then I'm using my key that she so graciously gave me.

*****

"Who is it?" I hear a man's voice. She must be back to getting dick now. She flipped to the other side again. *Make up your mind Nina. Now I see why you're so confused!*

"Mother Teresa," I replied in a real faint voice.

The door opens and it's my brother Terrance standing there. *What in the hell? This can't be life; the last person I want to see is him.* He's staring at me like he don't recognize that I'm his damn sister.

"Can I help you Miss?" He asked, gazing into my eyes as if they are familiar to him.

I know as soon as I open my mouth, he will know. "The question is…what are you doing here?" I asked.

"Lala? Oh my God! Why do you have that thing wrapped around your face like that?" Terrance dismissed my question.

"I was shot in my face fool! I'm sure you heard, bad news travels fast!" I said snappy. He should be telling me why he's at this bitch's house.

"Well nobody could get in touch with you since you changed your number and whereabouts! I didn't think it was that bad. Let me see!" Boy bye, so he can run back and tell his mother so she can gloat!

"Hell no! Are you going to let me in?" I barged my way in.

"Hold up, don't be pushing on me!" Terrance said as he shut the door.

"Where is she? NINA, NINA, I'M HERE FOR YOU, BOO!"

"Lala stop yelling! The whole building can hear you! Now what do you want with my woman anyway, and how do you know her?" His woman? Really Nina? Now I can see if you just went out and got you a little bang, bang, but she's in a whole relationship! Broke ass Terrance can't do nothing for her, but give her a baby! Please tell me I'm at a comedy show or something!

"Ha, Ha, Ha, Ha, Ha, Bro you are too funny! Woman, Ha, Ha, Ha, Ha, Ha! I'm gonna pee on myself! What happened to that baby mama you had? Nina was just sniffing in my ass not too long ago! Where the hell did you come from?" *Oh, my stomach hurts. This nigga thinks that Nina is his woman.*

"Sniffing? I don't believe that. Since when do you even like women? You a freak now? Fuck all of that, what do you want?" Terrance was quick to catch an attitude. *Nina done turnt this dummy out!*

"You over here all pussy whipped on a bitch that goes whichever way the wind blows! Go sit your corny, broke ass down somewhere!" I tried to brush past Terrance to go into the bathroom, where I heard the shower running. He grabbed me by arm with a heavy grip. *Now he's showing some strength.*

"Get off of me before I forget we run through the same blood!" I'm going to get to Nina and he's going to watch me beat her ass. Nothing like a good, old ass whoopin, especially when you're wet!

"Lala, whatever business you have with Nina will have to wait. Leave now before I throw you out of here!" Whew, bro thinks he can stop my show. Now this is funny. He better let me go before he finds himself in the ground sooner than he needs to be.

"I'm not going anywhere until I finish what I came here to do. You might want to leave, Bro! Don't want no blood to get on that new Polo shirt you rocking!" I'm packing after Moose shot me. I don't go anywhere without my main piece of steel. *If bro wants to catch a bullet then so be it! I wish he would just make this easy and let go of my arm!*

" Get out, bitch!" Nina finally decided to surface, gun in hand aimed straight at me. *This bitch wasn't in no shower, she was waiting on me.*

CHAPTER 14

JAY

Yesterday I took the kids to see Boss; it was family day at the rehab. He had no contact for the first couple of weeks, which was nothing new to us. We barely ever heard from him anyway. I'm proud of his progress thus far, still a ways to go, so we will see.

He was looking better already; his face was filling out and his skin color was coming back. He's still not the Boss that I met, but headed in the right direction. He played with the kids; there was a lot of laughter and jokes being thrown around. I just stayed to myself for the most part. A big part of me still resented him. Just some more pain that will subside, eventually.

We participated in group therapy; I only did it for the children. Anything to give them more of an understanding of what was really going on, and just how sick their father really was. Forgiveness takes time but kids are more prone to forgive than adults. They just let bygones be bygones. All they know is that daddy is back and getting healthier.

Now that Boss can be in touch with the outside world, he claims he will be calling every day. I don't doubt it. Rehab is like jail; it's when he gets out, that's when it will be show and tell!

*****

I was so drained mentally, physically, and emotionally though; I couldn't take anymore. I came home to Binky balled up on the couch with Grams consoling her. I still can't wrap my mind around her Uncle being killed. He was found in his apartment with one single bullet in his head, dead on sight! A man that never fucked with nobody, always stayed to himself! The only family that Bink has even known; a hard pill to swallow.

From what we know, the police have no leads. But Binky kept screaming out Moose's name, and then the money came back to me! All I can think of is, 'How is Binky going to live with the fact that her Uncle was killed at her expense?' Money; that green shit that brings out the worst in people. Dollars can always be replaced and will never amount up to a life.

I'm so sick of this street mess, that's reason why I'm not in B-more! I'm here to get a new start and get away from all of it! Not that the crime isn't happening here, it's different when you really don't know anybody and I don't surround myself with it. Another thing the kids had to deal with because they had grown so close to her for the short time she's been here. I already asked Grams to keep an eye on them while me and Bink make this dreadful trip back to dead man's land. I'm for surely not looking forward to it, but I can't let her do this on her own. We need to make funeral arrangements, most of which I can do from here. We need to clean out his apartment and get everything situated. All of this takes money that I don't have! If I would have known Moose was going to do this, then it made no sense for Bink to give that money back. I hope she texted him once she snuck it back it in there, like I told her to.

*****

Fred stayed here with us last night. Him and Bink slept in the living room, that's if she even got any sleep. I woke up a couple of times to her screaming and hollering. I'm pretty sure the kids and Grams did too. Thank God he was here. *I hope he comes with us to B-more to be of more support for the both of us.* Fred is a great guy and I can tell that he really has love for Bink. For the first time that I can see in her life, she really has someone that is for her. He's not out to hit and run, he's all the way in. These two have been kicking it strong, hanging out every day. This is the happiest I've ever seen her, well until yesterday. Now I've never seen her so hurt. There's no greater feeling than having the one you love there by your side to hold you up during these times of pain. I just hope she doesn't push him away.

*****

Work was just starting to pick up, but I had to cancel all appointments until further notice, not a good look for us! We were booked too. This was going to be our money week. Oh well, what can I do…stuff happens. There will be other opportunities in the near future. Right now we just have to handle this.

*****

"Jay, Jay!" Binky barged in the room.

"What's the matter?" Bink looked like she just saw a ghost. Her face was filled with horror.

"Mothafucker just sent me a text, read it!" Bink handed me her phone.

The text read: Yo, see you when you get here! I was down there looking for you. Had me playing hide and go seek! I was in Florida; you are in L.A.! See ya soon, boo. Unc will be missed! Love you, yo!

My hands started shaking, heart throbbing, adrenalin pumping. *Moose was some kind of a nut! Smart enough not to indicate himself though.* Bad enough he took an innocent life, but now you have the nerve to be throwing shots! I wish him nothing but bad luck. Karma will be coming his way. Whatever love I had for him was long gone. *I'm sorry, Jock, I know that's your boy, but if you were here, never in a million years would this be going on!* "I'm just done, change your number and now!" *Unc wasn't enough for Moose, it's obvious that he wants Bink too!*

"I can't go home Jay, now I can't even bury my Uncle and say my final goodbyes to him! This is just too much for me to deal with!" Binky ran and locked herself in the bathroom.

*****

I forced myself to get up, put on my robe and walk into the living room to talk to Fred. He was half asleep, poor man didn't get much sleep, dark circles all around his eyes. "Hey, you okay?"

"Yeah, I'm fine. Just a little tired." Fred yawned. "Jay, she's not doing well. All night long she's been blaming herself! I'm doing the best I can to try and keep her spirits lifted up, you know her better than me. I wish she would have just given that nigga back his money, but knowing him and his cruddy ass, he still would have done the same thing!"

"What are you talking about? I thought she gave Moose back his money! She was gone for a whole week, where did she go? Oh my God, I'm so confused right now!" Tears immediately started dropping from my eyes. Me and Bink didn't do the secrets between each other, no matter how bad it was. *I don't know how I'm feeling right now. Kind of betrayed, like how I felt with Lala. If Bink had of returned that money, Unc would still be alive! Now I know why she can't go back! This is all fucked up, Binky will never, ever, get past this!*

"She didn't feel like she could tell you, but I'm going to handle him! My baby knows Fred, but the streets know Woo, and this shit he's pulling up there don't fly this way! Y'all only know me as the Hypeman, the opener to get the show, but I got a lot of shit with me and bodies in the ground! My past ain't pretty. I do my best to leave it there, but when you fuck with someone that I love, the beast comes out in me! You and I both know that if Bink goes back up there it's not going to be a good outcome! She can't go, but you, me, and my posse can!" *Is anybody thinking? Killing Moose is not the answer. All everybody wants to do these days is cause pain on the next family. I understand the street code, but it doesn't mean that I agree with it!*

"Neither one of us has to go. If Bink still has that money then she can pay to have his body shipped here and we can have a private funeral. This way Bink will have a place to go to when she feels a need to talk to him." *Problem solved. Keeps us all out of harms way for a minute. Now I have to watch my back, the kids back, and Grams' back. Moose can't be trusted.*

"Dude needs to be dealt with. I do have a couple of shows scheduled up that way in between time I could just handle him then. Thanks Jay, I think that's a good idea. Just ship the body here, actually that's the only way we can do it! But what about his personal belongings?"

"I can call the Housing Authority and ask how much time we have? I'll just tell them that we are out of town, maybe they can bolt lock the place up. It's worth a shot."

“Well yes, just see what can be done, then we will go from there! Bink has been in that bathroom for a long time, let me go and check on her!” Fred brushed past me.

Chapter 15

Swift

Now that Diamond and I have made it official, my fiancé she is, and the planning has begun. We both agreed the smaller the better. Just something simple but elegant. I'm on some fallback stuff anyway. I ain't rolling with many. I'm a one-man army right now. Everything I do has to be planned out in a strategic way! With nobody really that I can trust to watch my back it's making things twice as hard. I been on some late night creeping trying to see how these niggas is moving. By now Moose should know that I'm out, and because I haven't looked him up, he already knows what's up!

Sweets put Diamond on his visitor's list, just like I asked him to do. She made her first weekly visit to inform him on what's going on with the plan. She let him know straight up that I needed some trusted help. He was able to set up a meet between me and Ole G! I have to see how this goes. If I don't get the right vibe then I'll remove myself! The meet was at Old Town Mall where wasn't no happenings. The place been deaded for some years now. At first I was skeptical, this would be a nice place to get myself killed, but I knew Sweets needed me out here to be his eyes and ears. I pulled up in my new black 320I BMW, a little something for now. My lawyer is working on getting them cars released. The Feds talking about they are a part of their investigation.

Ole G was already waiting on me in his old Cadillac. He wasn't what I expected. He didn't look like no old school drug dealer, more like a businessman, in his black suit and Stacy Adams on. Clean cut, nice build; he definitely took care of himself.

*****

"Hey Swift, nice to meet you! Sorry it's on these terms. My name is Leroy." He shook my hand.

"What's up?" I'm going to keep quiet and let him do most of the talking, that way I can see what direction I need to take.

"Sweets let me know that you need some help. I can provide that for you, we both have a common interest at stake. Your boy screwed us all, and I left my business to Sweets; I ain't been in this shit in over twenty years! Up until recently my money flow was pretty damn good. Right now it's being affected. I have a family to take care of and protect. Whatever you need to make this problem go away, I'm here for you." Dude was smooth as shit, Ole G had a swag to him to.

"Alright, alright, I feel you! For me it's more personal. Moose was like a brother to me and for him to do this to me!" I pointed at my chest. "Man, you can't possibly understand where I'm at mentally. I wanted out right before the shit went down. It was already in place for him to take over. I was leaving the state to go be with my girl and leave all this shit behind me. He didn't have to do this!" Anger was taking over and I don't think well when I'm angry.

"You don't think I haven't been in your shoes a time or two? Yes I have. It comes with the job. I wore the shoes that you are in. That's why I told Sweets that he better not put one finger on you; let you handle your own business. Swift, it wasn't just about you. He took down Sweets and Rock! Now as long as y'all been dealing, everyone always respected each other's territories. I think you three were the dynamic trio. There was no beef, everybody was getting money and that was that! The game has changed since I been in it, I get that, but loyalty should always remain the same. I got cats that I ain't seen in years, but if they were to see me right now I would still get the same respect that I did back then. Now a days you young bucks don't know nothing about that! Everybody wants to be the head man in charge, but everybody ain't built for it! I'll tell you what, those few that had the heart to try me, are no longer here!" *Ole G is the reason that Sweets called that meet. Now I get it. Everything is coming together. He gave direct orders. I knew it was crazy how all of a sudden Sweets came up with that bright idea. Sweets went from wanting to kill me to seizing all fire.*

"Yeah, I can attest to that, but I'm old school. I'm one of the ones that still go by the rules. Sweets had you, so it's natural for him. Don't know about Rock, but he got that old school in him too. We all were taking a hit anyway because of the pill poppers taking over. That's what's hot right now and none of us have access or a supplier. Shit been going downhill for all us lords! The money wasn't rolling in like it used to anyway, for real! Why did you get out?" *I want to go out on top just like Ole G. Live the good, clean life.* This man put in his time and let go. He's sitting back chillin, still collecting money, but I want all the way out. Just give me a lump sum and I'm gone; don't even call me for no consultation.

"I got out for my family. When you start having children you have to think better. I wanted to be around for them. My hands needed to be as clean as possible. When I had my first daughter I was out here in the streets heavy, and it caused strain on my relationship. Young, dumb, with plenty of bitches on both my arms. It was rough and I missed out on so much when things went sour between me and her moms. They were able to get into her head and make me out to be this fucked up father when that wasn't the case. I took care of her financially, but physically I wasn't around and it hurt me in the end. When I met my wife and she got pregnant that's when I started training Sweets to take things over. Only a fool makes the same mistake twice. Because I was vested then, I would always get my percentage, and he was okay with that! What was your reason for wanting out?"

"My woman. No kids yet, but she said, 'Swift, you're going to end up dead or in jail.' I let that marinate on my brain for a little bit and decided she was right! I made my money and was smart with it. She knew that if I would have stayed here I would never get out. We know too many people and you already know how this business is. I had to do some things that I'm not proud of, and I do have some haters, that one day may come after me!" *Yep, just like Rock said, he won't be happy until I'm dead. Well I can think of a few more that feel the same way as him.*

"Okay, young man! You think like a champ and I like that. Back to Moose. What do you know that he knows?" *Now I'm for sure, this man is a real Ole G.* He's thinking this out and asking the right questions. *Yeah, I'm in good hands.* If I had someone like him training me I wouldn't have got caught up in half the things that I did. For me it was a lot of trial and error. *Sweets has a good overseer. Much respect to that. Matter of fact, I salute him.*

"Well, let me put it to you this way…Moose isn't the brightest. There's no way he set us up all by himself. He may be running shit, but he has a silent partner; the brains behind all of this! He doesn't have the mind for it. The way I ran my operation was Jock handled anything pertaining to the shipments. He dealt with all the connects and supplied the crew. Moose handled all of the security operations. With Jock being gone, Moose took on the bulk of his responsibilities. I just had the final say-so. Other than that, I was the mastermind that made everything work together. Moose is good at protecting and mean with a gun! I knew when getting out of jail that there wasn't going to be no running up on him! From what I see going on, he's getting sloppy, and most likely because he's trying to do too much. I made the news; he's expecting me. He just doesn't know when I'm going to strike. I operate quietly, so if I'm going to come at him I have to do something where he doesn't think it's me!" This is where my help will come in at. Yeah, I could have ran up on a few cats, but if I have to question where you stand then it ain't even worth a shot. I need some sho nuff help.

"In other words, you need to come at him loud and clear. Is that what you're saying?" *Good thinking, Ole G, but I still have to be me.*

"Not really, he has a couple of houses and I need to be in one when he comes home. He's expecting me to meet him on the streets so I need to do the opposite. It ain't in my makeup to go to a nigga's home! That is where I need help. Moose has heavy surveillance surrounding his houses, and the dummy took some of the crew and has them outside his house wheeling and dealing, plus paying security!" *Nigga must think he so grand now. That shit wasn't like that before he set me up.*

"Give me the addresses, I'll have the surveillance taken care of along with the crew. I just need to do some checking. Give me a day. By tomorrow night I'll have a smooth sailing for you to get in one of these houses, as long as you don't mind staying in one until he comes!" Ole G gave me a yellow sticky note and I gladly wrote down all three addresses.

"That's what's up. Once I'm in I don't care if I have to wait a week! I just need to do this and get it out the way! Thanks man and I enjoyed our talk." I finally found someone who I want to be just like. *He don't know it, but he's my inspiration.*

"It will be my pleasure to know that the rat from the camp has been put to bed. May he rest in hell!" We gave each other that meaningful handshake from an Ole G to a Young Buck, as he would call me, knowing what had to happen was understood between us both.

Chapter 16

Lala

Dr. Miller said my surgery went well. Now I'm home recuperating, face burning like I was in a fire and itching like a bitch. The pain pills are helping, but when that shit wears off it's something fierce going on. I just have to keep my mind focused on the finish line, and that's half the battle. I'm waiting impatiently on pulling off these bandages, just a couple more days before my sneak peek. For the first time in my life I feel so lonely, no one to help me or cheer me on. I had to catch an Uber to and from the hospital. Good thing it wasn't anybody I knew driving.

Nina almost blew off my face by the time she fired. I ducked just in time. If I believed in God I would say it was him that saved me, but I'll take that credit. My face can't take another bullet. If she would have hit me I would have been a done deal. Terrance jumped in between us like he could stop a bullet, stupid idiot! Putting himself in that kind of danger between two women with guns. After that bitch missed, I had to try and draw on her, flashbacks running through my head of what Moose did to me. The only reason I didn't pull the trigger was because of stupid ass! I didn't come for him, I came for her and I was more than willing to test out my hand game. Guns never had to be involved. With the way he was protecting the pussy licker, it was either shoot him in the head to get to her, or walk away. I walked away…until further notice. Swift taught me that sometimes you have to chill on a nigga. You catch them while they taking a little nap and then you react. Plus, I was banking on Moose to handle my light work, but he didn't come through. He told me to handle it, that it was my business. *Since when?* As trigga happy as he is, I just knew that he would do it for me. Even after I told him that Nina had his houses robbed, he still went over there and collected his money and did nothing. *Times must be hard for him, poor baby!*

I'm willing to bet that Moose is running scared of Swift. Nobody has seen or heard from him as far as I know. That means that when Swift comes, he's coming hard. After watching Swift run his operation for years, I know how he thinks. Unless Moose doesn't know yet, but I'm sure somebody told him the minute he got back in town from wherever the hell he went. I wasn't going to bring it up. I need to save my own ass. The man already came after me once, Swift been wanting me dead. I wish there was a way to keep him from finding out that I had something to do with him being in jail. Somewhere deep down inside he has to still love me, even if it's just a little bit. *Maybe I can use that to my advantage.* The good thing is right now I'm not mobile and very few people know where I live. The odds of catching me out are slim to none. Well you know me, I do have a plan, always do. Once Swift gets rid of Moose and I have the pleasure of thanking him, then I can go get his bitch and use her to bargain Swift with my life. He let's me live and his twat can live. *Although I would love to know that she's rotting in the dirt.*

*****

Every bitch that has ever crossed me has suffered in some kind of way. Bink just lost her uncle, if nothing else broke her…this will. I'm waiting to hear about the funeral arrangements so I can send some black roses stamped with my name on them. I want her to know that I sent them. I don't know who killed her uncle, or why, because the man was always strange anyway. Nobody wanted to be bothered with him. I never felt uncomfortable around him; the way he would peek out the door looking at me as if I was some kind of an edible arrangement with his old ass, wrinkled dick. Now he could have got some for the right price, but he was broke.

I always wondered if Binky was fucking her uncle. A lot of strange shit was going on in them projects. Binky loved him dearly, like he was her man. Glad we ain't friends, I would have had to be there for her and shed a fake ass tear. I'll leave that up to Jay, and her sensitive ass. *Always the one with a soft heart.* From what I read in the gossip news, her life isn't going too well. Boss all strung out on drugs with lawsuits coming left and right from his artists. *See, if only he would have listened to me when I told him he needed a woman like me.* She drove that man to getting high; they both deserve it. Jay couldn't handle that man, she's too emotional. Life is hard, the key is to be harder than it.

*****

Mommy Dearest should be HIV positive by now. My father has a bad habit of picking up a trick here and there. I paid Kay Kay to go after him since he likes them young. Yes, that bastard took her up on her offer. Weak to some infected pussy. Hopefully it spreads to where I needed it to land. He can keep on creepin with my mother and still going home to his wife. Hopefully they both will catch of whiff of playing the fool for a man! Two old ass women going strong for over thirty years with the same ass man. For the life of me I can't wrap my brains around it. I might be able to deal with it if my mother was a kept woman, but hell, she has a bank account on E. Me and my brothers shouldn't have wanted for a damn thing, but we barely had the necessities. *Huh, nothing makes my skin crawl more than a stupid ass woman!*

*****

Diamond reminds me of my mother, just take the loss and move on with your life. That's probably why I despise her. She makes me sick down to my bones. Just find a lane and stay in it. Stop moving in mine. We been going at it since I took her high school sweetheart,

Donte. I saw how he was spending that money on her; had her rocking all the latest fashions and flyest hairdo's. She didn't deserve all of that, so I made my move on him. One day Diamond was home sick from school, which gave me an opportunity to do what I needed to do. I asked that nigga for a ride home, he was kind of hesitant, till I put my sad face on, fearing that Diamond wouldn't approve. It took a little bit of persuasion and peer pressure to convince him. Once I got in that car I sucked him off from here to heaven. That night he broke up with Diamond and I was riding in that car. You have got to know how to suck a mean dick and move them hips. Donte broke her little heart. She was crying all in the school. It was so sad and I was rubbing it all in her face. Holding his hand while he walked me to class, kissing him in her face. He was wide open for me. Every time she tried to charge at me, Binky handled her ass. I thought once he got caught up and went to jail that Diamond would be okay, but nooo. She's been holding a grudge ever since. But when is she ever going to get the fuck over it! She'll never look or be as good as me, it's just not in her genes. The best thing mom and dad did was create me. *Ugly is calling, what in the hell does he want?*

*****

"Yeah", I said not really in the mood for him.

"Yo what's up with those supplies?" I'll be glad when I never have to hear his voice.

"You should have them later on today." With everything going on, I forgot to put the order in; it's a day behind schedule.

"Later on today ain't gonna cut it. I need them shits now. The whole east is out! What the fuck are we supposed to do, lose sales now? If you can't even handle providing the sales let me know, I can have another bitch take your job!" *He's a stupid ass.*

"Go over west and get some to hold you over. Simple solution. It's not that big of a deal!" Duh! This dummy is acting like it's an emergency, and we never lose business…they just go to another one of our spots.

"Yeah, Yeah, Yeah, I could do that. You are good for something other than sucking dick and swinging your pussy! Good thinking. Listen, by any chance have you heard from Binky? I'm trying to figure out when her uncle's funeral is." *He's so disrespectful on all levels.*

"No I haven't. We don't talk, remember?" He got some nerve with his ugly ass self, rolling my eyes.

"I was just asking…no need to get all snappy and shit. Death brings people back together! You know what I'm saying, shorty?" *Yep, get off my phone.*

"Supplies should be there this afternoon, just send me a text when they arrive." *CLICK. No more words for him.*

Chapter 17

Binky

Today is the day that I say goodbye to my uncle. Jay made all the arrangements to have his body shipped here. I still had to go back to B-more; me and Fred flew in and out the same day. John Hopkins wouldn't release the body until I identified him. He looked at peace, but I wasn't. It was mind blowing to me. It just made it all so real. It was one thing to know, but another to see. I didn't do well. The whole hospital probably heard me screaming. I definitely made my mark in that morgue.

*****

Yesterday it was the same thing. Jay took me to the funeral home to give my final okay on how he looked, and I passed out; woke up in the hospital. Too much to bear. I know we won't live forever but it's how he died. It wasn't from a heart attack or cancer, he was killed, and I had everything to do with it. The doctor in the emergency room gave me a sedative, one that wouldn't harm my baby. The nurse came in the room to tell me that I was pregnant after they were running tests. She asked me when was the last time did I have my period. I couldn't remember. When they took me down to ultrasound is when I found out that I was twelve weeks. It's very possible that this baby belongs to Moose. Fred came just as I was getting the news. Him and Jay were jumping for joy. Fred automatically assumed that this baby is his, but I slept with Moose, then flew down here. Moose always uses protection but he was drunk as fuck and slipped up. I don't want this baby to belong to him, me and Fred gel so well. This baby would be both of ours first child. I don't know how I'm going to tell him that I'm unsure. I don't want to break his heart or cause that kind of strain on our relationship. He's ready to start shopping and get us an apartment of our own. His plan is to leave Monica and be with me full time.

All I know is that I'm about to be a mother and I have nothing but smiling faces around me. It's a hell of a difference from the last time I was pregnant and Lala was all frowned up, talking shit. I'm going to be a damn good mother. Unlike her, I get to think of someone else other than myself. *I hope that selfish bitch never brings a life into this world; baby probably be crying and screaming, while she's in the mirror prancing around looking at herself.* Oh yeah, I forgot about that bullet. Maybe she's fucked up for life! It wouldn't be a bad thing. I would love to see her right now, just so I could laugh in her shot up face! Kudos to whoever did it, I applaud them. Got her right where it hurts!

*****

"Bink it's about that time, the limo is outside." Jay came in the room to help me stand up and get me out the room. I had been just sitting on the bed, never paid the clock any attention. Didn't want to do this, but I had to. She held my hand as we walked out together. Grams and the kids were ready and waiting.

We were all dressed in black on a beautiful sunny day, that was so dreary on the inside. Everyone was just quiet as Jay motioned for them to come on and follow as we walked out to get in the limo. A ten-minute ride felt like an hour. I could feel the sadness without even looking at everyone. I just stared out the window until we pulled up to the funeral home. I saw Fred and Monica. *I asked him not to bring her. How's that gonna look? I haven't even told anyone about his situation. Jay just thinks she's a business partner, now what? I don't need all the extras right now. Fred has some explaining to do, and he better get her ass out of here!* He must have read my mind as he walked over to the limo waiting for me to get out. He grabbed me by the arm.

*****

"Baby she wouldn't take no for an answer, I did my best. We shouldn't have any problems. I'm here for you, and I'm not leaving your side." Fred wanted to be done with Monica ever since he found out I was pregnant, so either way he didn't care, but I do.

"No the fuck you won't! She's here so go tend to her. I don't want her saying anything to the kids, and you and her can disappear when we go to the gravesite. DON'T COME AND I MEAN IT!" *All I want is peace on this day. If I wanted havoc then I would have buried my uncle in Baltimore.*

I walked in with Jay's arm wrapped inside mine. She was looking back for Fred as I led the way down the aisle. Grams and the kids were following behind us. Unc looked good, better than he did yesterday. The funeral home did a good job. I noticed a lady sitting down and she stood up as we walked in. I'm a little leary, wondering if maybe Moose sent her because I've never seen her before and this was a private service. Immediately I become nauseous, as the tears just won't stop coming down my face. I'm stuck and can't move from in front of the casket. I feel Jay trying to pull me away so that I can have a seat. I yank myself back. I'm not ready to move, remembering the last day I saw him alive and the smile that was on his face when I was leaving. Unc was happy, even told me to hurry and get settled so he could come. *I had the money, why didn't I just bring him with me?* "Why, Why, Why?" I screamed.

Fred came running to the rescue, grabbing me and forcing me to sit down with Jay. I'm balling my eyes out, nothing but guilt filled me. My heart hurt likes it never hurt before. If I take all the pain I've been through and added it up, there still isn't any comparison.

If it wasn't for this baby, there would be no need for my existence. Right now all I want to do is be right beside my uncle in a casket; dead, where I can't feel nothing. *I hope you looking down on me Unc, knowing that I didn't do this on purpose. I wonder what Moose said to you before he put that bullet in your head.*

I guess it's over, Jay stood up waiting on me to get together. I was so zoned out that I didn't hear a word of anything that was said. The casket was closed with the flowers on top. *When did that happen?* Well, it's time to head to the graveyard...Unc's final resting place. As I was trying to gain my composure and find the strength to get up that strange lady walked up to me.

*****

"Hi Binky, I'm Loretta, Fred's mom. I'm very sorry for your loss. Can't say that I remember you or your uncle, but my heart goes out to you. I'm here for you if you need me." *What in the hell was Fred thinking? Now you have your mom here and we're supposed to be cousins. This woman doesn't know me from a can of paint. Why did he tell the lie to his mother?*

"Thank you Ms. Loretta, I appreciate that." *Please just go!* Thank God Fred came over and grabbed his mother. Jay had the strangest look on her face. *Now is not the time.* I managed to get up. As I was walking to the limo, Monica came over and gave me a hug, along with her condolences.

*****

The graveyard was only up the street. It was a short ride and Fred must have listened to what I said, there was no sight of him. It was short, sweet, and to the point. I handled myself well, as nothing but anger just resided on my face. No more tears, just pain that couldn't be controlled. My uncle was in his final resting place, but would forever be in my heart.

*****

Last night, Grams finished cooking a meal that we could come home to eat after the service. She made all my favorites, turkey, ham, baked macaroni and cheese, mashed potatoes, greens, yams, potato salad and buttery dinner rolls. Once the rolls were done and the food was heated up, we all started to grub. My appetite was coming back, I guess. For the most part we were all silent. I guess because of me. Normally when we eat there's always a lot of conversation going on, laughing and joking. I didn't feel like doing much of nothing. *I just want to curl up in the bed and sleep until the pain goes away.* After we ate Grams went off to her room. She was tired and wanted to rest. The kids ran off to their room, and that left me with Jay. I knew what was coming now.

*****

"Bink, are you okay? You're carrying around another life inside you. Too much stress is not good." *Doesn't she think that I know this already.*

"I'm good Jay, never been better!" I said sarcastically. *How in the hell am I supposed to be okay?*

"I didn't mean it like that. All I'm saying is the last thing you need right now is a miscarriage. If you think about that baby, then that should give joy." Jay put her hands on my stomach.

"This baby is the only reason, I want to live. I want to see what I created and experience motherhood. To be able to say this child belongs to me is going to be the one thing that I will always cherish. But I'm not sure if this baby is Fred's or not. It could be..." *I can't even fix my mouth to say that murderer's name.*

"Oh Binky, I thought he always wears condoms, afraid that some woman would trip him up!" Jay looked like she was all of a sudden sick. I am too, at the thought, but this baby is mine no matter the outcome.

"He does, but that night I got him drunk, he didn't have one on. Anyway I'm thinking about not telling Fred anything at all. He'll be the better father. Only thing is...will I be able to live with myself?" When I care about someone it's hard for me to continue on with a lie. Somehow I always end up telling on myself.

"That's a hard one, Bink. Wouldn't want to be in your shoes. All I can say is go with your heart. Just know that if you decide not to tell Fred then you have to take that to the grave. Don't get a bunch of people involved that could be potentially hurt. You have time to really think. It's not smart for you to decide right now with your emotions running high." *This is why I love Jay.* She got me with whatever I choose to do and I don't have to worry about her running her mouth.

"Thank you, Jay! I love you so much. If you were a dude we would make an amazing couple." *My first time laughing in days; kind of felt good to get a chuckle in.*

"Real funny, good to see you smile. Now what the hell is going on between you and Fred? Why was Monica with him and what was the deal with his Momma?" *Jay didn't waste any time getting down to the nitty gritty.*

"Something else I need to fill you in on. Fred's mom and Monica think that I'm a long-lost cousin on his dad's side. Monica is actually his girl that he lives with. It was just easier for us to do what we wanted without him being questioned." I figured might as well be all the way honest, no need in trying to cover up another lie.

"Wow Bink, why oh why? What's going to happen when you have this baby? Fred is still going to be cousin, and you're all up in that chick's house like it ain't nothing! This is so cruddy, nothing but drama. I thought we were getting away from all the trifling shit we used to do! We're supposed to be better than this, Bink. Damn, damn, damn!" *Jay is making it seem like this is the worst thing in the world. I really don't feel that bad. I've done worse. Shoot, I've been right up in the bitch's house sexing her man in her bed. Then have the nerve to walk by her and speak like it was nothing.*

"Fred wants to leave and come out and be honest. I don't want him to. Monica is helping us build up clientele right now. I can't let him just fuck shit up for us!" We still have to think about the business.

"You must have flipped and fell off a rollercoaster. Let me tell you like this, we won't have no clientele once this comes out. How many of them clients do you think will really fuck with us once she blackballs the hell out of us? What are you going to tell Monica once you start showing? Binky, leave that Baltimore shit that we used to do right up there. You came out here for a new start; physically and mentally!" *I know Jay didn't think that just because I moved, that I wasn't Binky. I'm still the same, just in a different place. I am who I am and that's what it is.*

"I just need for you to rock and roll with me on this until I figure everything out. Right now I can only deal with one thing at a time." *Jay needs to cut me some slack; did she forget what today was that quickly?*

"Rocking and rolling with you could have got my ass killed if Moose would have found us. Now you need to listen to me, bad decisions hurt your tomorrow. You already seen what happened to Unc, and that bag of money that you have wasn't worth it! You will not be sitting here hurting over me because of some shit that you did! I'm not going down for Binky and her bullshit! Unlike you, I have come too far. Yeah I had to turn a trick here and there to make ends meet, but I'm done! My focus is to get back on top the right way!" *I don't need no reminders of my uncle. He ain't been in the ground long enough. This is still all too fresh.*

"Jay, stop acting like this is out of your league, my memory works well. Ever since I been here, you been riding your high horses. Come down a few notches. You're a Baltimore bitch just like me and always will be. No matter how far you run!"

Chapter 18

Swift

"I don't want to get out of this bed." Diamond turned around hugging me from the back, butt ass naked.

"I know one thing, I'm getting tired of this hotel. We might need to find a furnished apartment with a short-term lease, like the college kids do." We don't plan on being here long, but in the meantime, I want to be comfortable.

"No problem, I can go look. I miss cooking for you, I need my own kitchen." Diamond jumped up and sat on the side of the bed.

"Yeah, a home cooked meal would do me right. Eating out every day ain't cutting it; I don't even have a taste for any takeout food." I rolled over and pushed Diamond back down on the bed.

"Stop it, Swift!" She laughed. "Are you ready for tonight?" Not a good time to change my mood from playful to serious business.

"Yeah, everything is all set for me to go in." This is the part I hate about the business. When someone crosses you, an example has to be made and it don't matter who it is…mother, father, brother or sister. If not, then you just a punk ass bitch out here, and it took me too long to gain my respect.

"I'm scared, Swift," Diamond said looking at her ring. "What if…"

"There are no what if's, think positive. I'm coming out that house alive, we got planning to do and places to go." I definitely don't want her worrying about me even though I know she will anyway. The more I assure her, the less she will stress.

"You're right, I trust you, it's just so dangerous. I wish you could just catch him on the street or something. You don't know what he has in that house." *I'm three steps ahead of Diamond.*

"That's already been taken care of. Ole G had some dudes on the inside to handle that. His word is bond, I'm good on that end." I'm not one to trust very easily, he has a certain persona to him that only somebody like me would understand.

"I'm going to start my day. Don't forget you have to meet that lady at the deli today for Sweets. He said be there at ten-thirty sharp." Diamond walked off to take her shower.

*****

The other day when Dime went to see Sweets he wanted me to meet up with the cook that works in the jail. I'm trying to remember who she is, but I can't picture who he's talking about. We're meeting up on Calvert St. at this small deli spot. She's giving me some instructions on what he wants done. He should have asked Ole G, I don't work for him, only with him because of this case. *Nigga is not going to be trying to call the shots for me to do shit for him. I have enough on my plate to handle. Sweets needs to be put in his place.* I'm no one's piss boy, setting up meetings like he got it like that. Every time Diamond goes to see him it's something else. He just ought to be grateful that I let her visit him. We can't trust the phones, them lines be recorded. The only way to keep him up to date is a visit. Since I have to meet this cook, let's me know he has an outside contact. If he keeps this up, I'll just inform her and she can relay the message. I don't know what he's up to, but I need my mind right for tonight. No distractions is a must and here he goes messing with me.

*****

"Alright babe, I'm off to take care of a few things. What time should I expect a call from you?" Diamond asked nervously.

"Don't stress, Dime, I'll text you once I'm in there and call you once it's all over with. I love you and it's me and you forever." I said, pounding on my heart.

"Love you, call me throughout the day please. I need to hear your voice as much as possible." *That's my baby. Wouldn't trade her for the world.*

Time for me to take my shower and head out to this meeting.

*****

She better be here and on time. I walked in the deli, got me a jar of orange juice and sat at the back table. The place was empty; only two other guys were sitting in there. The door opens and in comes this big ass snowball looking woman looking around. *This has to be her.* I cleared my throat for her to look my way. She turned around, looking at me giving me one of them seductive smiles. *Sweets better had sent her for business purposes only.*

*****

"Are you Swift?" I nodded my head and motioned for her to have a seat directly across from me. She sat down in the chair, out of breath, with both sides of her ass hanging off.

"Yeah, what up?" I asked.

"Well it's good to finally meet you. I was the one hooking y'all up when you were locked down." *Am I supposed to say thank you?* This full breed white woman acted like she had some black in her. She was white on the outside, but the minute she opened her mouth she made me think I was talking to a sister.

"Oh yeah, you made them pancakes?" That's about the only thing that was good to me.

"Yeah that was me!" She squirmed and chuckled. "They call me Heather with all the feathers, cause I make some mean chickens too."

"Okay, so what does Sweets want?" I'm not trying to have no conversation with the woman. *Just get to it.*

"He told me to ask you for some cash, cigarettes, and weed. Sweets said that you could handle it." Seems like she chuckling after every sentence. *Nothing is funny. This shit ain't cool.*

"How in the hell does he expect for me to get that in there?" Let me listen to his bright ideas. It better be good or else it's a, 'Hell to the No!'

"I'm going to wrap it all up in Ziploc bags and put it up in my pussy to smuggle it in. Don't you worry, I got this man." *I'm putting money on his books, why all the extra?* This is just some dumb shit to have his ass caught up catching another charge.

"Don't they check you when you go in?" Home-girl don't need to be losing her job.

"Yeah, that's why it's going to be up there!" She pointed in-between her legs. "Anything for my man!" she smiled.

Oh wow, he's hitting that. "I'll see what I can do. You have a number you can jot down on this napkin?" It took her a minute to find a pen, then she jotted down her number.

"Just hit me up when you have it. I'll be around, cutie." Before she could get her big ass up I was out the door. *Sweets is off the chain. He was banging that to get what he wanted; a much better man than me.* I can't subject myself to certain levels, but everyone likes what they like, I guess. He should be smart enough to be flying straight. I'll bet my last dollar that Ole G don't know nothing about this. That's why he had her come to me and not him.

*****

Nightfall came quicker than I thought. I waited until I got the text from Ole G to make my move. Getting in Moose's house was no problem. I snuck in through the back door, which led me straight to his basement. I walked up the stairs and had a seat on his couch, staring at his PlayStation, ready to break it. I texted Diamond as promised, didn't even look at her reply. When I'm in situations like this, all I need to concentrate on is everything that Moose did to me, how he turned on me. His intentions were to let me rot in jail, after all me, him and Jock been through. I peeped out the window to make sure that I covered and I was. The guys were all out front, instructed to make sure that Moose was not strapped when he enters his house. Courtesy of Ole G, a big thank you to him. They should be able to handle him real quick before they throw him in this door. I stood up, starting pacing back and forth. Two hours have went by and no Moose. *Wish this nigga would hurry up and catch this death sentence.* Just as I'm thinking, the fool pulls up. *Good.* I hear some rumbling going on outside. Sounded like the fellas were doing the job. The door opens up and in comes Moose, being thrown flat on his ass.

*****

"Hey there, brother!" The sound of my voice has him shook and off guard, just how I wanted him to be. He struggled to stand up and turn my way.

"Swift! Hey man, what's up? I been looking for you. Heard you was out and didn't even look me up! I'm so glad you're out, these streets is getting rough out here!" Moose made it sound good, almost believable, if I didn't know any better.

"Nigga, you know why I'm here, and you also know why I didn't come see you! Why try and set me up?" *I know I shouldn't be talking, but I feel the need to get some answers.*

"Man, I didn't set…"

"Shut the fuck up with that bullshit! You cut everybody off. Had dudes stepping to me while I was in lockup looking for money that was promised to them! Changed your number because you didn't want to be contacted, so what's really good?"

"Man, I had to. The Feds was all up in my shit! I couldn't have nothing or nobody connected to me, if I wanted them off my ass! I had intentions on getting everybody back right, it ain't what you thinking!" Moose was patting his pockets like he was looking for something. *Yep nigga, you ain't strapped.*

"Nah, I'm not buying into the fuckery! There was other ways to get around that, you and I both know that! Cut the shit, why did you turn on me? I'm going to give you about three seconds to come up with something real good before I blow your fucking brains out!" I pulled out my gun ready to fire off.

"Damn, you're going to kill me! Old punk ass Swift came over here to end my fucking life, had me hemmed up outside so now I can't even defend myself. What you scared to give me a fair one, or you knew you wouldn't stand a chance? You just gonna draw on me and shit! It don't matter what I tell you, you're still going to shoot, coward ass! You had them dudes out there turn on me since you did that tell them to give me back my shit and we can face off nigga!"

"Ain't no face off nigga, now you want a fair one! It's a little too late for that shit. Did you give me a fair one when you had me walk in that warehouse? Fuck no, you thought you had this all in the bag, but you ain't that smart! You dumb as fuck, sorry greedy ass!" *This nigga got the balls of a horse. He already knows how this story goes.*

"Nah, that would be you. Your bitch told me how you was getting over on me, how you were planning to take me out of the business. I just beat you to the punch, simple as that!" *Now I'm getting somewhere.*

"What bitch you talking about?" Please Diamond, don't tell me you had something to do with this.

"Your bitch, Lala, the one that you ran behind like a sucka. Yeah, she told me everything even about you hitting that cunt Binky behind my back! I ain't the grimy one standing here!" *Lala is in the mix once again. This bitch just doesn't know when to stop.*

"You believed that shit coming from someone like her? Man, you knew she had it in for me, I kept you and Jock up on that tricks every move. You allowed that bitch to string you along with a bunch of made up lies! I was handing you over everything, the business was all yours, fool!" *Leave it to Moose to fall for some shit. Jock would have saw right through it.*

"Yeah right, if that's the truth, it's only because Jock is no longer here. I always felt like the third wheel. That's why I had to get rid of Jock. You should have heard him screaming like a bitch. It took me a while getting that head off!"

"NOOOOOOOOOOOOOOOO! Lights out Nigga! *POW, POW, POW, POW, POW, POW, POW, POW, POW, POW!* Ten bullets straight in Moose's head.

Chapter 19

Lala

Thanks to Dr. Miller my face was at fifty percent. Applying a lot of makeup pretty much covered up my scars. I learned from watching Jay. Now I can get out and about! My mirrors were back up and all my hijabs were in the trash. Dressed in all black with some black leggings hugging my fat ass, a black, tight tee shirt with my nipples at a stance and my black Nike's keeping it simple, but sexy as all hell. When I hit the streets I'll probably cause a few accidents and arguments just because all eyes will be on me. It's just a joy to be me and I respect the hate; it's to be expected. Scarred and all, I can still can run circles around these bitches.

*****

I tried calling Leroy a couple of times. He's probably mad at me for not returning his calls. It's been months since I last spoke to him. We weren't on good terms anyway, since I made that visit to his house. I was only calling to get some dick, but oh well, there are others out there more than willing to bang this up! After being locked up so long my love life is empty and needs some fulfillment.

*****

Bitches I'm back and I know a few that won't be too happy to see me! I'm so looking forward to some unofficial visits. It's time to let my presence be known, and I'm not to be fucked with! I still have my key to Nina's house; hopefully she didn't change the locks. It's early so I know she's still sleeping, and that's exactly how I'm trying to catch her. She don't get to shoot at me and think that I'm going to just let it slide. *No sir, not me. There will be no repeat offenders of Moose.* Bitch could have ruined me for life. She knew what I went through and how I felt. Now that she's getting dick, it's fuck me! Bitch I made you! This come up got so real that she thought she could take over!

I had to laugh as my key went right in and unlocked the door. *Not too bright Nina. The first thing you do is change the locks, but thank you for making this easy for me.* As I was doing my walk through I see my brother Terrance's picture on the wall. *Oops! Well what do you know...it came crashing down.* I expected to see one of them come running out of the room from the noise of the picture, but it was nothing but silence. By the time I reached the door all I heard was bunch of loud ass snoring. I already knew who that was. Terrance used to keep me up at night, never got too much rest. The only way that I could sleep was if I was already asleep and hoped like hell I didn't wake up in the middle of the night. Anybody that can sleep through his snoring is a true champ. *Aww, look at the new couple cuddled up together. Nina with her pink nighty on, half of a butt cheek hanging out!* I walked over grabbed her ass and stood back. She just moved her ass closer up on Terrance. I see why these chicks be going crazy over my brother, he's packing. *Well that didn't work, I'll just go back out and sit in the living room and watch some TV until the lovebirds wake up.*

*****

Made a pit stop in the kitchen, opened up the fridge, saw this nice, big, juicy apple that I could munch on. Hmmm Nina must have just went shopping, the fridge was stocked like we were having a snowstorm in the summer. Time to get comfortable on the couch. Flipping through the channels there wasn't anything good on to watch. If the show don't have anything to do with shopping or fashion, it doesn't hold my interest. What about some music? Yeah, that sounds good. Something I can dance to. My jam is on. Before I let you gooooo oh oh oh. Damn I still got it, grinding in the mirror just a jamming!

*****

"What the hell are you doing in my apartment?" Nina yelled over the music.

"Now we had our good time, that's what they say, we've been hurtin each other…" I was singing.

"Look bitch," Nina turned off the music. "You got some nerve coming in here turning on music and singing like you're at a damn concert! Get out and leave my key. Stop trying so damn hard! I don't want you anymore!"

"You look good in that pink nighty honey." I was still dancing around grinding to the music that was no longer playing.

"Keep playing Lala. I'll wake your brother up and let him deal with you!" Nina said that as if Terrance would make me jump or something.

"You see my face, almost back to normal! Come on and celebrate with me!" Whew I had to stop, I was getting out of breath. *My workout plan will be starting back up. Can't be getting all out of shape.*

"Yep I see it, makeup does wonders. You're still the ugliest human being I have ever met in my life! You no heart having bitch! I used to stick up for you and say that you were just complex, but that's not it! After talking to your mother and both your brothers, I have a real clear picture of just how ruthless you really are!" Nina was walking towards me.

"I'm glad you got that off your chest? Is there anything else you would like to say?" Whatever Nina needs to say, she might as well get it all out.

"Just leave before I stomp the shit out of you!" *Nina is big shit now, threatening me.*

"Okay, have it your way!" I pulled out my steel. Nina screamed and try to run back to the room. *I hate having to shoot a bitch from behind, it's not a nice thing to do. BOOM! BOOM! BOOM!*

"What the fuck? Oh my God, Nina get up. Get up Nina! NINA!" Terrance came running, yelling and screaming from the top of his lungs. *Wish he would shut up already, she's dead.*

"Calm down, Bro. Get yourself together and act like a man, for once! Put some damn clothes on. I don't want to see your naked ass!" *I see he woke the hell up!*

"Lala, you did this shit. You shot Nina!" My brother looked at me with tears in his eyes while he was holding Nina. *Blood was everywhere. I never seen anyone bleed this much and fast too.*

"Get up baby, I'm going to get you some help! SOMEBODY CALL 911. CALL 911!" He's yelling like these people in this building actually give a damn. Just some more gunshots that they hear every day, all day.

"Shut up Terrance. Ain't nobody calling nobody. In this neighborhood this is the norm. She's bleeding pretty bad." *I don't think she's going to make it.*

"Shit, where is my phone? I have to find my phone. Stay with me baby, stay with me!" Terrance ran back in the room looking for his phone. *That must be his phone that was sitting on the living room table. I saw it when I was sitting there. Nina's phone was always decorated in leopard print, her favorite.*

I bent down picking up Nina's limp hand. Have to be careful not to get any blood on me. "She's dead, Terrance. There is no pulse." Well that was easy, especially for someone that only had target practice a few times. Yep she's a goner. "See girl, you shouldn't have been fucking with me like that!" I whispered in her dead ears. My first dead body, I knew I could do it. All these years I been wanting to kill someone. Yeah, this can be kind of addicting. Feels pretty good to be rid of a problem.

"She's gone, my baby is gone! Ohhhhhhhhhhhhhhhhhhhhh she's gone! I'm never going to forgive you for this. It will be a long time before you see any daylight, you just watch! Your crazy ass needs to be locked up somewhere!" *Aww, poor brother, stumbling over his words; just pitiful. Please dry up the tears. All that 'mommy dearest' put me through and he ain't never cried like this over me. They say blood is thicker than water, I can't tell. I'm feeling like I'm the damn water.*

"I knew you would turn on me. She shot at me and instead of you whooping her ass you continued to fuck with the pussy licker! I'm your sister! I told you before, that you never had my back! Now you're talking about snitching!" *Boy you better think this is Baltimore, snitches get stitches. He will end up dead in an alleyway.*

"I can't even think straight right now! My God, My God!" He's a bloody, naked mess. *Bro ain't taking this too good.* "I can't stand your wicked ass. There wasn't too much that I wouldn't have done for you. Saved your hot ass on a many occasions. Niggas & bitches had it in for you, but no, what did I do? Took it them that's what. Wasn't nobody laying a hand on my sister! I should have let them eat you alive, and Nina would still be here because there would be no you! You don't know what I did for you behind the scenes; it wasn't your business! You ruthless, dick sucking, pussy eating, Bitch!" *Don't he know I'm armed and dangerous! You shouldn't talk to people any kind of way when they have the power of your life in their hands.*

"Well it would have been nice if I would have known, not that I believe you anyway! You're just a cornball, always have been." I shrugged my shoulders.

"I'll show you a cornball, you ungrateful whore!" Terrance threw me on the ground like he didn't just see what happened to Nina, touching me with his bloody hands. The sight of blood being on me makes me squirm. *Let me put this Nigga to bed!*

Chapter 20

Binky

Jay has been acting funny towards me ever since I told her the truth. I been trying to keep my distance, hanging with Monica and Fred more these days. I get up early and go to the boutique to help out Monica when I'm not booked doing hair. What I need to do is buy me a car and get my license. Time to grow up. These cabs are pretty expensive.

I do my clients' hair out of their homes when Fred is busy. He can't cart me around from place to place. Finding a car should be the easy part; it's the licensing part that scares me. DMV takes you through too much, class after class. If the process is real crazy, I'll be driving around illegally. I don't want nothing fancy, just something to get me back and forth. A car that don't cost no more than five g's; damn sure don't want no car payment.

Money is still not a problem for me. I'm penny pitching. A bank account sounds nice, but I like to see and feel my money. *In my black bag it is.* I don't use that money unless I have to. With a baby on the way I can't afford to be broke. *That scum's money will take care of this baby.*

*****

Running a business by yourself gets hectic when you can't afford to pay for any help. Monica said she enjoys my company. When it's slow we end up just chatting it up like two sisters. When Monica finds out the truth, I hope one day we can be cool again. She's a beautiful person inside and out, a rare gem. Nothing like the rest of these tricks out here. Fred sure knows how to pick them. If he knows like I know, he will make it work with her. Even though I know his heart is over here with me, I'm much different from Monica. She's so not street smart, a typical girl that came from a middle class family. Monica doesn't know what it's like to struggle and worry about a meal. She comes from a two-parent home. That alone is a miracle in itself. Her parents have been married for over twenty years. She has a brother and sister that are both in college getting a degree. *Now that shit ain't normal.* I know she's the black sheep, being a mother of two. But even with her being a mother, she still has her own business at twenty-six, not too bad at all. She did tell me that it's family friction going on; her parents wanted more for her. Unreal. *She's doing better than most of these hoodrats out here. They need to be thanking God that they didn't have a daughter like me, then again my life would have been very different.*

*****

"Binky, what's on your mind? You looked spaced out." Monica asked, reminding me of a lot like Jay.

"Just thinking. I have some stuff that needs to be taken care of. I'm considering getting my own place, kind of scared to step out there on my own. Need my license and a car." *Now that I have a baby on the way there's just not enough room. Jay is already sharing her room with me as it is.*

"Oh, I can help you with that. It's kind of expensive doing it all by yourself, but as long as I keep throwing clients your way, you should be just fine. Tomorrow I'll have a list together for you and I can take you to DMV to get the paperwork started. Have you been looking for somewhere to live, or are you just throwing out there?" Where I want to live will sound real crazy right now, so I'll keep it to myself. *Back to the hood I go. I miss it, and if I can't be in B-more, then so be it. I'll take what I can get.* The hood keeps me on my toes. These uppity neighborhoods are boring, and cost too much money to live in.

"Not yet, I'll start soon. Once you give me that list I can start checking out the neighborhoods. How is it being a single mother?" *Just need a little bit of insight. Seeing it and going through it are two different things.* Jay got them kids after the fact, and this baby is mine, stuck with me till death do us part. People are quick to get married, but a real marriage is with that child. That's if you plan on being there.

"Why? Are you thinking about having a baby? Binky, listen to me, wait until you have that special someone that's going to be there. You don't want a baby daddy. You want a father. A man that's going to be there with you every step of the way. I was going through hell before I met Fred. My baby daddy wasn't shit and I was too stupid to see it. He dogged the hell out of me. When I first told him I was pregnant, he ran. I didn't see him again until my daughter was three months. He came back with this sob story about how he was scared and realized that he made a mistake. I believed him, took him back for the sake of our daughter. Plus, I still loved him. I wanted us to work and I was determined to make it work. My parents cut me off because I took him back. I had no help at all. Things were going good between us, so I thought, but I was doing everything by myself. All he did was help me pay the bills. I woke up tired and went to bed tired. When I got fed up with him doing everything he wanted to do, I decided I was going to put some of the responsibility on him. I told him he had to pick Destiny up from daycare, and every other Friday I was going out to do me. Well the Friday that I was supposed to do me, he left her at daycare and I haven't seen him since. Three weeks later I find out I'm pregnant again. He doesn't even know about Malik. I still haven't seen him."

Wow, this is a horror story. I would have beat his ass after the first time. No second chances running around over here.

"That's crazy. What about his family?" No matter what the struggle will be, I'm open arms for my child.

"Girl please, they cover for him. They don't want no part of my kids. They're just as sorry as his ass. My kids have Fred. His mother stepped in and took both of them under her wing. She's their grandmother. I know you're related on his father's side, but his mother's side of the family, all of them are real cool. They treat my kids just like they are family. If I didn't meet Fred, I don't know where I would be. You see this boutique, look around, Fred helped make my dreams come true. Before him I was a single mother struggling to make it, about to lose it all, and he stepped in and saved the day. I had just lost my job, and was headed back to the welfare line. We're still kind of new, less than a year in, and I'm ready to get married, have him adopt my kids. I want it all with him. I love him so much and I can't wait to have his kids." This chick is talking about marriage and adoption. Honey you moving in the wrong direction. Fred is on the left side of the street and she's on the right. Delusional thinking at it's worst. Let me pick her brain for a minute.

"Have you told Fred all of this?" Just wondering if he has he been lying to me.

"No, he's been acting a little strange lately towards me. He's still showing the kids all kind of love; he just seems to be distant. Like, it's weird, he's going through something. We haven't even been having sex. I try to touch him and he's either too tired or not in the mood. Most men can't wait to hit it. Usually, it's the other way around. He was sleeping the other night, girl I rolled over starting touching and caressing him and he didn't even get hard! He's having problems getting up, but all he has to do is talk to me about it. I'm in this for the long haul. I'm thinking about slipping him some Viagra just to make him feel better about himself. All he has to do is communicate with me and together we can work this out. Has he said he anything to you?"

Damn ain't nothing wrong with his dick, it's working just fine. Fred might have to fuck her, at least every now and then. He don't even know how to play it off, and her stupid ass never once even thought about him cheating. I'll never have that kind of trust for a nigga. "No, Fred doesn't talk much about you and him. We mostly talk about family stuff, but I'll see if I can pull anything out of him." *Well Fred, you are on the up and up, telling the truth. First real nigga I ever met.*

"Thank you, Binky. I appreciate anything you can do. Fred is my heart and soul, girl." Monica hugged me.

"I have a little secret to tell you. I'm pregnant. That's why I was asking about being a single parent!" *Sooner or later she was going to find out.*

"Binky, by who? Let me guess, that thug in Baltimore? Oh, Oh, Owwww!" Monica was grabbing her hair. *Bitc,h it ain't your problem.*

"Yeah, I haven't told him yet, and please don't say anything to Fred yet." *Fred is going to be pissed. He wanted to tell Monica. I hope she don't run her damn mouth.*

"I won't, but you better tell him. I can't have you going through this by yourself. Why don't you just move in with us? I know what it's like to be pregnant alone. It's a bad feeling, Binky. Anything I can do to save another woman, I will do." *Hell no, then I wouldn't have any privacy with Fred. She's dead ass serious too.*

"Naw, I need my space. That's the whole reason why I want to move out now. When I do move, I know y'all will be there for me. If it gets too rough then I will consider it." *She's such a sweetie.*

"Girl, you need money. You can't afford an apartment, car, and a baby. Just think about it please, at least until you have the baby! Wait, how far along are you?" *Jay just texted me and told me to get to the apartment ASAP!*

"I have to go Monica, will call you later! Jay needs me, like right now!" I ran out the door without realizing, *How am I going to get there.* I'll call a cab and have them pick me up while I'm walking.

CHAPTER 21

SWIFT

I'm back handling these streets like I never left. Shocked the hell out of most, made quite a few changes. Getting things back in order the way they should be. Keeping my word to Sweets and Rock with no funny business. All of us had our territories back, with me just overseeing their money and operation, with the help of Ole G. Between the two of us, we pretty much had things running smoothly in a short time. But not without putting a few knuckleheads in their place that thought they were going to buck. Yeah, they claimed they wasn't doing nothing unless Moose told them to. That quickly turned around in my favor once they found out there was no longer a Moose. That was all it took for them to see things my way. I wasn't playing no games. Your ass could be eliminated.

*****

I straightened out Rock's family. They were pretty bad off; facing foreclosures, cars being repossessed, bills backed the hell up. I fronted some of my money and would repay myself in increments, keeping a tight record of every last dime. For a family that hated me, they damn sure acted like they loved me once they were able to eat again. I was getting treated like a God. Not a damn one of them mentioned Tiz. No matter how good they treated me, I still wasn't trusting them, so when Rock's mom offered me some dinner, I turned it down. As good as it smelled, it could have been the fake out. They needed me though, to stay afloat. Rock had the nerve to send me a thank you through one of his cousins.

His books wasn't looking too bad either. *Once I pay myself back I'm going to stash some dollars away for him too, show a nigga how you save some damn money. Never spend every dime. Just as fast as you get it, is just as fast as it can go. Always have something for a rainy day.*

*****

Ole G basically was handling Sweets' dollars. Other than me feeding Heather her supplies that she was smuggling in the jail, I didn't have much to do on that end. Ole G was calling all the shots. All I was doing was delivering the messages to the fellas. He was behind the scenes. As it stands now, he only meets with me. A temporary position until he picks one to handle the head man in charge. With all my responsibilities I barely have time to breath, trying to stay on top of everything. It's all good though, I'm getting my left and right hand ready to take this shit over.

Worm and Rahim are in training, and they don't even know it. Two of the realest, that I think have the business, plus street mind to take the east off my hands. They remind me of myself. Built with the same morals and loyalty. Every day the bond is getting stronger between us. These sleepless nights are soon to come to an end. All I need to do is get to a comfortable place, where eventually I can make my exit.

*****

The drug game has paid me. I did what I set out to do; conquered and I'm tired of it. Never thought that I would ever feel this way. Seen too many niggas behind bars, buried too many niggas in the ground, got too many bodies with my name on them. I still got this court shit hanging over my head. Shit ain't the same for me anymore. No more excitement. I saw firsthand what power and jealousy does to a weak-minded person. Moose turned on a nigga that would have took a bullet for him, killed him, chopped his head off and left his head on my car. To this day that sight goes through my mind ten times every day. He tried to put all of that on Lala, but he already had it in for me and Jock. He killed Jock way before that crooked ass set up even happened. Moose was already making moves, all Lala did was strike a match that was already lit. Let's see if she puts out this fire while I'm lying on her bed quite comfy staring at her picture smoking a much needed blunt.

*****

"Who the fuck is in here? Whoever you are, you better come out before I smoke this motherfucker out!" Lala was yelling. *Well let me get up and entertain her with my presence.* I walked out and stood there in her hallway.

"Well hello slut, how the hell are you?" I laughed. *This shit was amusing.* Looking at her busted up face, covered in make-up, looking like she just saw a ghost. She dropped her grocery bag, grabbing her pocketbook.

"Swift, how did you find out where I lived? I didn't send for you, so why the fuck are you over here? Furthermore, how did you get in here? This particular slut hasn't changed one bit, just a tad bit worse.

"It wasn't hard. You had some dealings with a co-worker of mine, and he knew exactly where you lived at. I can get in any where that I want to." Ole G spilled the beans. Once I mentioned her name, he gave me all the info that I needed.

"Old faithful ass Moose, I'm glad his ass is gone. Thank you for saving me the trouble, but I really wanted him to suffer!" *Lala got a good grip on that pocketbook; she has something good in that thing.*

"Nah, he didn't have time to give me your address, but he was able to fill me in on some bullshit that you fed him. This meet and greet between us to has been a long time coming, don't you think?" *What did I ever see in this empty bitch. I admit I had some blind moments in my life.*

"Leave me alone, Swift. I'm not playing no games with you! What's done is done. I need to get ready to go to Moose's funeral, which you could have paid for, by the way, since you set it up to look like a robbery, leaving his family to come up with money to cover the expenses." *Yeah right, I already paid the price for Moose.*

"Don't try and change the subject, I'm not talking about Moose, and what makes you think that you will be living to make it to the funeral?" I have a feeling she will be making a later entry, if at all. It just depends on how she carries this convo.

"It crossed my mind a thousand times, and I know for sure that if you really wanted me dead and gone, then I would be. You had plenty of time to come for me, but I wasn't your target. I had to put my thinking cap on and really just sit back and evaluate." *Well, what do you know, the bitch uses her brain.*

"Smart thinking. You know I'm a man of my word, and I promised your brother that I would let you live on the strength of your mother and the rest of the fam. I heard he's no longer here because you took him out, meaning you're no longer covered underneath your family brand!"

"Excuse me, you don't know what the hell you're talking about!" *Yeah, I must have struck a nerve.*

"That's what you think? I always know what I'm talking about! The funeral you need to be worried about is your brother's! Some kind of sister you are. No mercy on your own flesh and blood! I wonder what the cops would say if they got a little inkling of a double murder. Can you imagine yourself in jail for the rest of your life, like you tried to do me? Now that would be interesting. How long do you think you could last with the big dogs? You lucky I'm no snitch, but don't push me! You were always cold, but baby you're a block of ice now." *Lala changed, well no she didn't. The fake wore off.*

"What do you want, Swift?" *Lala was nervous as hell. It's so funny how the table turns.*

"That's just it, what do you think I should do to you? I could kill you, but you're soul is already gone, no real justice there. I could blow the other side of your face off, that won't do me any good! You're already ugly as fuck! There's nobody else for me to get at. You don't give a damn about nobody! You ran off the people that actually gave a damn about your trifling ass! You tell me what is sufficient enough?" *Watch something stupid come out her mouth.*

"After all that you've done to me, that is what's sufficient enough! What, did you come over here to get your dick sucked or to tell me that you still love me?" *Suck, love, she's crazy as hell. The love been gone and Diamond handles this dick very well.*

"Your nasty ass was trying to play me in these streets. Diamond stepped to me and I did what I had to do. I'm glad things turned out the way they did because she showed me what real was."

Lala can't stand the mention of Diamond's name. *The jealousy is real!*

"Whatever Swift, you and your bitch can go to hell!" *That's what I thought, no real comeback.*

"Not before the dirtiest bitch alive! I could send you there now, but why should I when your life is already hell! Damn, hell ain't looking good on you at all! I see right through that makeup. Reminds me of a terrorist attack!" *Got to hit her where it really hurts, let her know she ain't all of that!*

"I've just about had enough of you, motherfucker! Keep talking and you will end up like Terrance, meeting Moose at the bottom of the dirt! This ain't the old Lala you fucking with! New and improved, you bitch ass nigga!" *This bitch just threatened the wrong one. She thinks I'm going to give her a chance to get in that pocketbook of hers. Nah, not that stupid!*

"Ha, ha, ha, ha, ha! You crack me up, running around here thinking you somebody! You think that gun in your pocketbook will save you? Wrong, wrong, wrong!" Worm grabbed Lala from behind and put her in a headlock as I was walking up the hallway towards her. Yeah, I had my backup with me, hiding in the kitchen, in case she tried to get stupid, which I knew she would. *Ms. Trigger Happy, thinking she could just kill everybody. Dumb bitch!*

"Listen here, slut," I grabbed her by her face while Worm still had her on lockdown. "Stay the fuck out of my business, leave my crew alone. If I find out that you contacted them or my suppliers again, then I will blow your fucking empty brains out! Go back to sellin that ass for money, that's what you're good at! Have I made myself clear?" Lala was still calling herself trying to run things, getting involved in my business, talking down to the crew when they already had specific orders not to pay the bitch no attention.

Lala nodded her head but that wasn't good enough for me. I let her face go so she could talk. "I can't hear you!"

"Okay, just tell him to get off of me!" She said as if she was begging. Being in a headlock is an uncomfortable feeling. Good for her, she ought to be thanking me that I'm letting her live.

"Oh one last thing I must do before I leave here!" I spit in her face three times. That was the best feeling in the world. "Worm I'm gone, do what you want with her! She sucks a mean one. If I were you, I would fuck her in the ass first then make her clean your dick off with her tongue! I'm just saying, if it was me! Oh, and don't let it get too good to ya, that you start sleeping on her, she will try you!" I walked out with her purse, leaving Worm to have it his way with her.

CHAPTER 22

JAY

Boss has been out for two days with no where to go, other than here. I got him a blow up bed so he can sleep in the living. Binky is staying in the room with me and that's the way I like it. Clean or not, I'm not going backwards, only moving forward.

He's been spending time with the kids, trying to make up for lost time I guess. With hearts of gold, they are enjoying him, so far, getting something they never got, Boss was being a father. It's like he's back to his old self, but the resentment that I have in my heart from the life we used to have is sticking strong. Can't get it to let up, on top of the jealousy that's setting in. Now that he's acting like he has some sense, the kids seem to be ignoring me. I'm used to helping them with homework, playing games with them, and getting them ready for the next day. I'm trying hard not to take it personal, he's been absent for so long, and to finally have him with a healthy mindset is giving them hope. *I can't help to think, how long is this going to last?* The kids don't need another let down in their lives. I'm grown, I can handle me, but I need to protect them. Now that Boss was clean and sober he finally gave me that genuine thank you for stepping in and raising his kids. I appreciate that because I needed to hear it. *Finally got the recognition that I deserved from him.*

*****

All hell broke lose in B-more, Ms. Agnes, Grams' best friend called and told her that Moose was found dead in his house, with multiple gunshots. I had to break the news to Binky, wasn't sure how she would react. I sensed some relief from her, almost as if justice had been served.

Bink and Fred drove up to B-more to clean out Unc's apartment. Time was winding down anyway. Housing Authority only gave us thirty days to have everything cleaned out.

*****

The next day we got another call from Ms. Agnes telling us that Lala's brother Terrance and his girlfriend were also found dead. The detectives were saying that it was drug related. I've never known Terrance to be out there like that, but it's been awhile since I seen him. I remember when he was crushing on me and I was crushing on him. Lala wasn't trying to hear it. From what I knew, he was a decent man. All the people we grew up with were dropping like flies, with no murder charges being given. I still don't have a clue who killed Jock. That's the life in B-more; everybody keeps their mouths shut. *Somebody had to see something.* Nine times out of ten, it's handled in the streets. *Glad I'm away from it all.*

*****

"Hey Jay, can I come in?" Boss was at my room door.

"Sure, what's up?" He opens the door, comes in and sits on the end of my bed.

"I'm getting ready to go to my meeting, but I have a couple of things I want to run by you. I'm working on getting back in the studio, all I'm feeling right now is music. The beats in my head just won't leave me alone." *Okay he's been home two days and already wants to go back to what brought him down.*

"Not a good idea. Don't you think you need to straighten out some bad blood first?" *Boss owes and people want their money, not a damn beat.*

"That's how I'm going to do it. I need money to pay all the artists that I owe, and it ain't gonna come from the sky. If I get in the studio and drop some beats that the label loves then it's another payday for me. I can get them to upfront a payment. Look, this addiction that I have is normal. I'm not the first producer that got caught up and I won't be the last. Second chances don't come easy, but my talent is undeniable. Everything that I touched went platinum. Jay, I need this. I can't just lay around here waiting for a meeting every day." *Selling dreams is all I've been listening to all my life.*

"Seems like you have it all under control. I'm going to sit back and stay in my lane." Once a mind is made up, ain't no changing it. I'm not wasting my breath. Instead of Boss focusing on becoming stronger, he's worried about what made him weak.

"The other thing I want to speak on is us. I know you don't trust me and are not all in with me. I expected you to welcome me home with open arms. My counselor warned me that this would happen. My addiction caused me to lose sight of you. Contrary to what you may believe, I love you, Jay, and I always have from the day I laid eyes on you. I messed up bad and I'm man enough to admit it. The drugs is the cause of me acting outside of myself, and every day of my life from here on out, is going to be a fight. It ain't over yet. I don't want to do this alone. When I was in the rehab, I filed papers for a divorce from Tasha. Like you, I have no idea where she is, so it will hit the newspaper, and if she doesn't respond then it will be granted. I'm serious about getting every part of me together. You are one of a kind. They don't make them like you anymore. Whatever it is that I have to do to make this right, it's on and poppin, baby! I can't fix the past, but I can damn sure make the future brighter!" *A day late a dollar too short, as the old folks say.*

"I know they told you not to make any promises just yet. My heart has been stomped on over and over again. The love that I felt for you, I'm not sure if something like that comes back. I have never in my life loved someone the way I loved you. I can say this because I've also never experienced this kind of pain either. The deeper the love is the stronger the pain. Boss, I've been hurting all my life. When I met you, there was happiness where that pain subsided deep within me. It was like all that pain just disappeared, only to come back with a vengeance. You can't guarantee me that you'll never get high again, you can't guarantee me that you'll never hurt me again. You already promised me the world, and gave it to me for a minute, only to take it all away! As sick as you are, you're even sicker in this moment. Coming at me after only two days of being home! See if you feel this way or are talking this talk a year from now. You don't know how low I had to steep just to keep these bills paid!" I said, as the tears rolled down my face.

*****

Back to the Commandments of a Female Hustler! The story of my life! No matter how much I try to escape that life, it always finds a way to come back! The brainwash of Lala still lives on!

Other Books by Stacey Fenner

THE COMMANDMENTS OF A FEMALE HUSTLER

Available at: Amazon

Meet the well-known trio, Lala, Binky and Jay, who been rocking and rolling together since their childhood days. Raised in the projects these three had only one thing on their minds, the come up! These ladies will show you how to use what you got to get what you want!

What starts out as 'may the best woman win' ends in a rage of jealousy, dividing the three. After such a betrayal, can their relationship be fixed? What happens when the commandments are no longer followed? One will find love, one will end up behind bars, and one's mind is sick and twisted!

Swift, Jock, and Moose have the east side of Baltimore locked down with the drug game, but stuff gets twisted when there's a murder involved. When relationships fail, sex, lies and love take over. Their loyalty towards one another will be tested in the worst way. Rivals will meet, love will be found and hearts will be changed as the hustler game is taken to a whole new level of disrespect!

Who will be the sell out?

*****

A TOXIC LOVE AFFAIR

Available at: Amazon

Tyrone and Daniel are two best friends but total opposites. Tyrone has his woman at home taking care of the kids while he's out playing in the streets. He soon finds out that being too comfortable and secure will cost him everything when he comes home to an empty home.

Will his womanizing ways wreck his life or can he get it together before it's to late?

Daniel on the other hand, is still trying to heal from a messy divorce with Candace five years later. He's tried dating but finds it hard to move on.

Find out what happens with a good-looking man who has money to buy everything but is unfulfilled on the inside. A Toxic Love Affiar is filled with love, lust, hate and drama.

*****

A TOXIC LOVE AFFAIR 2

Available at: Amazon

They say once a good girl is gone she's gone forever, and if you thought Part 1 threw you for a loop, then get ready to do figure 8's this go around.

Belinda sets out on a mission to destroy all her childhood, so-called, friends that have betrayed her. She has no boundaries or limits to her destruction. She has intentions on making each and every one of them pay, and has masterminded a plan that will eventually cause her to self-destruct in the worst way!

Being disloyal to Belinda will cost them everything. Everybody likes to play but nobody wants to pay!

Meanwhile, Daniel finally opens himself up to love again after going through his messy divorce with his scandalous ex-wife, Candace. That won't last too long when a jealous Candace gets wind of the relationship; she throws a monkey wrench trying to exhaust him of all hope. Meanwhile, Daniel is stuck cleaning up the mess Tyrone created.

Find out if Tyrone and Daniel's friendship can survive the aftermath when Daniel gets wind to what Belinda is up to and he feels responsible for her trifling ways. Shocked is an understatement as to how he feels about a woman he once had so much respect for.

Read and see just how toxic these relationships become!

*****

A Toxic Love Affair 3

Available at: Amazon

These toxic relationships will take it to another level of trifling in this final installment of the Toxic Love Series.

Tyrone takes a trip back down memory lane and reunites with his drug-addicted mother on a quest to find out who his father is. After hooking up with Dana, Daniel's sister, Tyrone decides to turn in his player card and be a father to all of the children that he has fathered, but karma has a funny way of landing right back in his lap.

Getting what he gave in life; will trouble from the past overcome him?

Daniel relocates back to Atlanta to be with Shaunda, the woman that he plans on spending the rest of his life with, but an unexpected visitor will come along and be the interruption of everything. Meanwhile, Shaunda reveals another side of herself that has Daniel questioning her pure existence. As Daniel's hatred toward his ex-best friend, Mr. Tyrone himself, grows after he learns of the secret relationship of Tyrone and Dana.

Sheree and Calvin's marriage is on the rocks once again because of Sheree's obsession in finding Belinda to seek revenge. Sheree bites off more than she can handle when another secret of hers is revealed.

Belinda makes her way back to the states and right back into the arms of her protector, Troy. But of course not without a twist to her madness.

Rivals will come face to face when a funeral places everyone in the same location...but who will meet their untimely demise?

*****

NEW HAVEN RATCHET BUSINESS PART 1

There's a lot that goes on in the small city of New Haven. Where the men have it their way, and prey on a woman's weaknesses!

Let me introduce you to the Bum Squad, which consists of Poncho, the ringleader, Rich, Quan, Mickey and Trey! Ladies, stay away from these types of men! Bums they are. They don't work, but manage to have all their needs and wants supplied by the women that they choose to date! These five men have it all with nothing to give!

Poncho is the dirtiest of them all, reeling women in, only to suck the life out of them, leaving them broken-hearted and confused! Rich, the washed up has-been finds himself stuck in a family affair that will have two cousins at each other's throats! Quan, Mickey, and Trey seem to understand their lane. They're not looking for much, just a place to lay their heads!

Liz and Chris are archenemies, both having a history with the infamous Poncho! Poncho does Chris in, leaving her suicidal and bitter! Liz runs to the rescue to dig her out of the pit of hell that she's mentally in!

Dominique and Keisha will face off over Rich and his lies of deceit. A gullible Mika will find herself involved in the trifecta love affair, as she becomes victim to Rich and his lies!

Find out what happens in the Ratchet New Haven Business.

About Stacey Fenner

Instagram: authorstaceyfenner
Twitter: sfenner1
Facebook: www.facebook.com/authorstaceyfenner

You can contact Stacey Fenner at
authorstaceyfenner@gmail.com

Stacey Fenner was born December 1 and raised in New Haven, CT., the youngest of three. In 1999 Stacey relocated to Atlanta, GA where she resided for a year before moving to Baltimore, MD to care for her parents with her two daughters.

Writing since she was a child was a way to express herself, allowing her to overcome many trials and tribulations. However, she never pursued her gift until 2008. Although she obtained her degree in accounting, and currently works in that field, her passion is and always has been writing.

Stacey's writing career is focused upon novels about relationships. Her first book, A Toxic Love Affair, which was published in April of 2015, landed her in the #37 spot on the Woman's Urban Best Selling list. Her follow-up novel, A Toxic Love Affair Part 2, landed in the # 24 spot on that very same list. Having just recently finished up Part 3 of that series, Stacey is taking the Indie world by storm.

Made in the USA
San Bernardino, CA
10 March 2018